DREAMS
INTO
DEEDS

Also by Linda Peavy and Ursula Smith

Food, Nutrition, and You
Women Who Changed Things

Linda Peavy & Ursula Smith

DREAMS INTO DEEDS

Nine Women Who Dared

Charles Scribner's Sons · New York

The publisher wishes to thank the following individuals, organizations, and institutions for the photographs used in this book: p. 13 top, Swarthmore College Peace Collection, Swarthmore, PA 19081; bottom, Brown Brothers, Sterling, PA 18463; p. 27 top, Brown Brothers, Sterling, PA 18463; bottom, Daniel Kramer; p. 44 top, Frances Collin; bottom, photograph by Erich Hartmann, courtesy of Rachel Carson Council, Inc.; p. 61 top, Michigan Historical Collections, Bentley Historical Library, University of Michigan; bottom, The Schlesinger Library, Radcliffe College; p. 79 top, United Electrical, Radio and Machine Workers of America; bottom, United Mine Workers of America; p. 95, Girl Scouts of the U.S.A.; p. 113 top, Library of Congress; bottom, Neg. No. 334024 (photo: A. DiGesu) Courtesy Department Library Services, American Museum of Natural History; p. 130, The Sophia Smith Collection (Women's History Archive), Smith College, Northampton, MA 01063; p. 142, Lamar University, Beaumont, TX.

Copyright © 1985 Linda Peavy and Ursula Smith

Library of Congress Cataloging in Publication Data
Peavy, Linda S.   Dreams into deeds.
Includes index.
Summary: Recounts the lives of nine determined women
whose achievements helped reshape the world.
1. Women—United States—Biography—Juvenile literature.
[1. Biography] I. Smith, Ursula. II. Title.
CT3260.P45 1985   920.72'0973 [B] [920]   85–40295
ISBN 0–684–18484–2

1 3 5 7 9 11 13 15 17 19   F/C   20 18 16 14 12 10 8 6 4 2
Printed in the United States of America.

To the dreamers of today,
the doers of tomorrow

Contents

Preface

In shaping the stories we told in *Women Who Changed Things*, our first book of women's lives, we became more and more aware of the fact that before there was a woman who dared to change things, there was always a girl who dreamed of doing so. It was an intriguing concept. There was a little girl . . . and she grew up to be a woman. And what she did and thought as a child had much to do with what she did and thought as a woman.

Swept by this idea, we decided to write a book that would show how the girls who dreamed became the women who dared. The women in *Dreams into Deeds* all grew up to do daring things, things that made the world better in one way or another. And because of their accomplishments, because they dared to be different, they have all been named to the National Women's Hall of Fame.*

---

* Located in Seneca Falls, New York, the town where Elizabeth Cady Stanton launched the movement for women's rights almost a century and a half ago, the Women's Hall of Fame was opened to the public in 1979 as a national monument to the achievements of outstanding American women.

But where did they learn that daring? Where did they get the courage to change the world for the better? They began by dreaming of a better world. And since most of their dreams began in childhood, we wanted to capture the dreamer who became the doer, to capture the spirit of the woman as seen in the girl. In order to do that, we decided to pinpoint a single, telling moment from each woman's childhood, a moment that gave some hint as to the direction her life would take.

We started with facts discovered while researching the woman's early years, then used our imaginations to flesh out those facts. But ours were highly informed imaginations. For example, only after reading all available materials on Rachel Carson's life, plus all of Carson's own books, did we begin to know the woman well enough to imagine her as a child, to imagine how that child would have reacted to news of winning *St. Nicholas* magazine's Silver Badge award, and to write a scene that captured all of that. By taking the facts we knew about a particular incident and adding details we could imagine from what we knew of the personality of Rachel Carson, we were able to recreate a moment that tells much about a little girl who dreamed of becoming a writer and who grew up to be the woman who dared to write *Silent Spring*, a book that changed our way of thinking about the world in which we live and taught us the meaning of the word "ecology."

By recreating a scene from Carson's childhood, we were doing something more. We were showing that these women of achievement were flesh and blood women, women who, as little girls, dropped to their knees on a muddy bank to watch a water bug, shared such moments with friends and parents, and behaved as if they were ordinary people. For they were ordinary. Yet they were extraordinary, too, in that they dared to dream, to set goals based on those dreams, and then to do whatever it took to accomplish those goals.

The dreaming came first, for nothing is ever achieved unless it is first imagined, and the women in this book could not have accomplished what they did without first dreaming of what they hoped to do. Thus in the fictional-ized vignettes that open each chapter, we have shown the dreamers—Jane Addams having her first glimpse of poverty; Mary Harris watching British soldiers destroy her family's home and hopes; Margaret Mead recording the words and actions of her two little sisters; and Mildred Didrikson pounding out the home runs that earned her the nickname "Babe."

But mere dreams were not enough. Dreams became deeds only when the women dared to do whatever was necessary in order to accomplish their goals. And so in the biographies that follow each vignette, we have shown the doers—Jane Addams moving into Hull House and being a good neighbor to Chicago's poor; Mother Jones teaching the workers of America the power of collective strength; Margaret Mead proving that the observation of primitive societies can teach us much about our own; and Babe Didrikson Zaharias breaking world records on her way to changing America's attitude toward women in sports.

We invite you to read of the dreamers and the doers, of the ordinary little girls who became the extraordinary women. And when you have read the stories of these nine women who dared to change our world for the better, we invite you, the dreamers of today, to become the doers of tomorrow.

1

She Dared to Be
a Good Neighbor

As the buggy rolled down the dusty rutted lane, seven-year-old Jenny fell quiet. She loved these trips to Freeport with her father. She was especially proud that he liked her company well enough to ask her along, and she knew that before they started home there would be some small treat for her from the sweet shop.

Freeport was much bigger than Cedarville, and there was so much more to see and do here. But her father had turned away from town, and now the buggy bumped its way down a street she'd never seen before. It was narrow, unpaved, and crowded with drab and dingy houses.

Jenny grew strangely uncomfortable. "Father," she said, tugging at the coat sleeve of the man beside her but not taking her eyes off a ragged child who was tracing lines in the dirt with a stick, "this isn't the way to town."

"No, it's the way to the mill, Jenny. I have some business out here that I have to see to first; then we'll go downtown."

1

As the buggy rolled slowly toward the large sawmill at the end of the street, Jenny moved closer to her father. Did people really live in these houses where doors hung off their hinges and windows were broken? Suddenly three children dashed from behind one of the houses and ran alongside the horse for a few paces, then peeled away and stood staring after them.

The carriage rolled into the mill yard. "You can wait here," Jenny's father said as he tied up the horse. "I'll just be a minute."

Jenny shifted around on the buggy seat so she could look back up the street. The three boys who had chased the buggy were now throwing rocks at a pile of sawdust not far from where she sat. She knew they were probably trying to get her eye, but she ignored them as best she could and turned her attention to a girl sitting on the broken steps of the house closest to the mill yard. She was playing pat-a-cake with a baby in a dingy nightshirt, but her eyes were on Jenny and the carriage.

Without warning, the baby pushed himself up on unsteady feet, teetered, then toppled over onto the rough boards and began to cry. Both girls were embarrassed by his screams, and Jenny was relieved when her father, true to his word, reappeared, climbed up beside her, and headed the horse back down the street. As they rolled out of the mill yard and past the girl holding the baby, Jenny smiled, but the expression on the girl's face never changed as she stared woodenly after the slowly moving carriage. Confused, Jenny spun around and stared straight ahead, holding tightly to her father's arm as they bounced along the

*rutted street and past the ramshackle houses that made her
so uncomfortable.*

*"Why so quiet?" her father asked when the buggy ran
smoothly over pavement again.*

*Jenny hardly knew what to say. "Those children have
no place to play," she began. "And how could anyone
live in those awful little houses?"*

*"Well, people do live there. Not everyone can live in
big houses, Jenny, or have nice places to play. Those
people can't afford to live anywhere else."*

*Jenny sat for a moment, thinking of the solemn eyes
of the girl who could never afford to live anywhere else.
Suddenly she turned to face her father squarely. "When
I grow up I'm going to have a big house, not where all
the other big houses are, but right in the middle of a lot of
little houses, and I'm going to invite all my neighbors to
use my house and my yard."*

*And that was, in fact, what Jenny did. For when Jane
Addams grew up she founded Hull House right in the
middle of one of Chicago's poorest districts, and her house
became the center of life for thousands of families around
her.*

Jane Addams, called Jenny by her family, was born on
September 6, 1860, in Cedarville, a small village in
Illinois. Her father, a wealthy and influential man, was a
friend of Abraham Lincoln's, and one of Jenny's earliest
memories was that of seeing her father cry at the news
of the president's death.

Her childhood was touched by tragedy of many sorts, and, perhaps because of that, she was a quiet child, shy and serious. Mrs. Addams died when Jenny, the youngest in the family, was two years old, and the little girl grew very close to her father. She wanted always to please him, yet she thought of herself as hardly worthy of him. Born with a slight curvature of the spine, she walked with a limp that was barely noticeable to others but which made her think of herself as an ugly cripple. So determined was she not to have her strong, handsome father associated with such an unattractive daughter that she would stand by her uncle during Sunday services, then walk home by his side after church, supposing that she could make the villagers think that only the three handsome older Addams children belonged to John Addams. Unaware of her feelings, her father saw her for the bright, attractive little girl she was and delighted in her.

When John Addams remarried, life changed abruptly for seven-year-old Jenny. Her own sisters and brother were much older than she and had never really been her playmates. The new Mrs. Addams had two sons, and George, the younger one, was Jenny's age. Together they played imaginative games in the fields around the large white house where they lived and walked to and from the village school.

Jenny was an outstanding student. From the time she had first learned to read, she had been excited about books, and by her late childhood she had read every book on the shelves of the small village library. Her father, himself an avid reader, was very proud of that accomplishment, but her stepmother insisted that books alone were not enough and saw to it that Jenny gave attention to art and music as well.

After high school, Jenny wanted to go to Smith, a girls' school in the East that offered a college degree, but at age 17 she gave in to her father's wishes and followed the example of her older sisters by enrolling in Rockford Female Seminary, a boarding school close to Cedarville. Though homesick at first and disappointed that she was not at Smith, she soon came to love Rockford and the friends she made there. She studied Greek and Latin, science, math, English and American literature, and religion and found the work challenging. She was president of her class and editor of the school paper.

All through her years at Rockford Jane Addams knew she wanted to do something important with her life, to live, as she put it, "to high purpose," but she was not sure just how she was to achieve that goal. For a while she thought perhaps she should study medicine and practice among the poor, and after she finished Rockford in 1881, she moved to Philadelphia and enrolled at Woman's Medical College of Pennsylvania. But her father's sudden death that summer had left her without her steadiest influence, though not without a comfortable inheritance. In Philadelphia, she found that she did not enjoy her studies, and when she suffered recurrent back problems later that year, she withdrew from medical school and returned home. There her brother-in-law, a physician, convinced her that surgery could cure her spinal curvature. Though the operation was a success, her recovery was long and painful, and she had many months in which to think about what she would do with her life.

In 1883, still uncertain of her direction, she traveled to Europe with her stepmother and came by chance across an area in London's East Side that reminded her of the poverty she'd seen years before in Freeport. The hopelessness of people who slept in the streets and ate rotten food discarded by merchants recalled to her her childhood vow to live among the poor.

Though she returned to the United States with some sense of what she wanted to do, she still had no idea of how she could do it. Aimless and troubled, she spent a frustrating two years warding off her stepmother's attempts to spark a romance between her and her stepbrother George; then, in 1887, she traveled again to Europe. More and more convinced that all her studies at Rockford had taught her very little about the real world, she returned to London's East Side to see life at its roughest. This time Ellen Gates Starr, a close friend from Rockford days, was with her, and together they visited Toynbee Hall. Rising out of the squalor of London's slums, Toynbee Hall was a residence run by church and university people to provide community services for the city's poor. For Jane Addams the search was over. By now nearly 30 years old, she finally knew what she was going to do with her life and how she would do it.

She and her friend Ellen returned home, and by 1889 they had moved to Chicago, a city of over one million people, three-fourths of whom were immigrants from Russia, Poland, Italy, Ireland, Germany, and other European nations. Having left their homelands in the hope of finding a better life in America, they had ended up living in crowded tenements and working for poor wages under inhuman conditions in Chicago's steel mills, stockyards, and factories.

Jane Addams went to the city in search of the big house that stood among all the little houses, the big house into which she would invite all her neighbors. It didn't take her long to find it. In an area where Halsted Street ran between the dingy stockyards on the south and the ship-building yards on the north, stood a decaying mansion. Built 40 years earlier by Charles Hull, a wealthy developer, it had once stood by itself, surrounded by green lawns and gardens, on the edge of Chicago. But now the city crowded in on all sides, and the mansion seemed overgrown by the array of tenements, saloons, and factories that had closed in around it. The neighborhood was in decay; the streets were littered and unpaved; homes were without sewer facilities and, in some cases, without water; neighborhood schools were inadequate and overcrowded; and there were, of course, no parks or playgrounds.

The upper floor of the dilapidated mansion itself had been divided into many small apartments, while the large rooms on the lower floor were used for factory storage. But Ellen Starr and Jane Addams saw that the house could be converted into a fine "settlement house," a place where they could settle in and spend the rest of their lives living and working among the poor. They had seen Toynbee Hall in London, and they had heard of a similar settlement house in New York City. Their house on Halsted Street could also become a center from which they could try to make life better for the people around them.

The two friends secured a lease, set to work with scrub buckets and paint brushes, and by September of 1889 had moved into Hull House. All the while the neighborhood was watching with great curiosity, unable to imagine what was going on, why anyone who did not have to would want to live on Halsted Street. But Jane Addams knew why, and she waited patiently to gain the trust of the people with whom she had chosen to live.

She did not have to wait long. Early one morning shortly after they had moved into Hull House and made known their willingness to be of service to their neighbors, she was awakened by a knock on the door. A worried young mother stood on the doorstep, a crying infant in her arms. Her babysitter could not take the child. Would the women of Hull House be able to watch the infant until she returned from work? It was all Jane Addams could have asked for. She wanted Hull House to serve whatever needs the neighbors had for it, and obviously day care for the children of working parents was a pressing need. Within weeks there was a day-care center at Hull House.

A kindergarten came next. From their experience with day care, the women could see the value of early childhood education, yet the local public schools offered no kindergarten classes. Obviously, Hull House should start one, and Jane Addams invited Jenny Dow, a friend of Ellen Starr's who had a special interest in young children, to move in and set up classes. Though Jane Addams's name is the one most often associated with Hull House, in great measure the success of the settlement can be attributed to Addams's ability to interest other people in joining her work. Through the years she surrounded herself with people who shared her interests and who frequently moved into Hull House and became a part of its work. One of these residents, physician Alice Hamilton (see Chapter 4), expressed what many of the others felt when she said that Hull House was the most exciting place in the world to live. As many as 50 residents lived there at one time, and as new problems arose, caring people were always on hand to help solve them.

Sometimes problems were discovered in unusual ways. To celebrate their first Christmas on Halsted Street, Jane Addams and Ellen Starr gave a party in the large parlor that just months before had been a factory warehouse. People came from blocks around to meet the women and see their house. Special candies had been set out for their guests, and the hostesses were somewhat puzzled to notice that many of the young girls politely declined the treat. When questioned, the girls explained that the candies came from the factory where they worked long, tedious hours, and they could not bear the sight of them. That Christmas party was the beginning of Jane Addams's lifelong crusade for labor laws to protect both children and adults, a crusade in which Hull House resident Florence Kelley played an important role.

When laws couldn't be changed fast enough, Addams helped workers in other ways. Shortly after the settlement house opened, the young girls who had been laboring under inhuman conditions in a shoe factory in the neighborhood gathered their courage and went out on strike. They demanded better wages and shorter hours. But the owner was able to break the strike by holding out until the girls were completely out of funds and had to return to work in order to earn money for rent and food. Sympathetic to their cause, Addams started the Jane Club, a boarding house near Hull House where young working girls could live cheaply while doing what they could to build a better life for themselves. And if they were on strike, that meant living at the Jane Club rent-free until the strike was settled.

Jane Addams also turned her attention to young children who spent endless, aimless hours on the street. She brought boys to Hull House for meetings of the Heroes Club, where they enjoyed afternoon snacks and stories of great men of adventure and achievement, men after whom they could pattern their lives. But club meetings and hero worship were not enough, and Jane Addams knew that. She remembered her long hours of play in the green hills around Cedarville. Here in Chicago, as in the milltown on the edge of Freeport, children played in trash-littered streets and alleys. With the help of Hull House resident Julia Lathrop, Addams successfully pressured city officials for the money needed to build Chicago's first public playground down the block from Hull House.

The trash-littered streets caused concern in many ways for Jane Addams, for she knew unsanitary conditions were likely the leading cause of her neighborhood's high rate of death and disease, particularly among infants and children. Because garbage collection service was so irregular, streets, alleyways, and yards were littered with decayed and dangerous rubbish. Jane Addams got herself appointed a city garbage inspector, and for a year she rose at six every morning to follow the garbage wagon, making sure that the men did a thorough job. As she had expected, the neighborhood's health statistics soon improved.

Addams knew the value of political power in bringing about change, and she did not hesitate to make herself a candidate for office to achieve her goals. There were 3,000 more children in the Hull House area than there were classroom seats to accommodate them when Jane Addams was elected to serve on Chicago's school board. From her new position she exerted the pressure needed to obtain more and better schools for her neighborhood.

She asked even more of the city in attacking another problem. Street crime, especially juvenile street crime, was widespread around Hull House. Children, sometimes through need, sometimes through boredom, got into trouble with the law. Once arrested, no matter what their age, they were tried and punished in adult courts, though it was common knowledge that children's special needs were not served by the adult system of justice. With the help of Louise Bowen, a prominent civic leader who lent much support to Hull House, Addams established the first juvenile court in the United States.

But Jane Addams's concern was not just for the young people of her neighborhood. She gave equal attention and energy to working with the adults around her. To help the immigrant families of Hull House neighborhood to feel comfortable with the big house and with their new country, Jane Addams opened her parlor to social gatherings several evenings a week, hosting German, Italian, and Irish Nights where neighbors came in to share the ways of the "old country." From these weekly meetings Addams realized that her neighbors not only needed to celebrate what they had left behind, but also needed to become more involved in American life. With the help of resident Grace Abbott, she converted some of the rooms of Hull House into classrooms for night school in language and citizenship.

Jane Addams also added a large kitchen to the old mansion in order to hold cooking classes designed to help the women of her neighborhood learn to prepare nutritious meals for their families. But convinced that their own foods were much better than the American recipes they were taught at Hull House, the immigrant women soon turned the special kitchen into a coffee shop where their neighbors gathered on their way to or from work or during the day to enjoy some special Italian or Polish or German or Russian dish. The Coffee House became Jane Addams's favorite example of the way Hull House worked. She had intended the kitchen to serve her neighbors in one way, but the neighbors themselves changed the project to meet their real needs.

Those needs were many and varied, and as Hull House grew it added a library, a branch post office, a gymnasium, an art gallery, a theater, classrooms, and meeting halls. Within a few years of its opening, there were as many as 2,000 people a week involved in its activities. Twenty years after Jane Addams and Ellen Starr moved into the old house of Halsted Street, Hull House had grown to include 13 buildings covering an entire city block. And those buildings were the center of life for the people who lived in that area of Chicago.

Though Jane Addams used her own finances to support the work of Hull House in its early days, she was able to persuade many influential people from across the nation to contribute the vast amount of money needed for the proj-

Jane Addams at 6

Jane Addams of Hull House

ect's growth and maintenance. Many of these, such as Mary Rozet Smith, Jane Addams's closest friend and companion, offered emotional, as well as financial, support. But despite the vast network of people dedicated to the work on Halsted Street, Jane Addams herself remained the primary reason that Hull House became the most famous and the most successful of all the settlement houses that sprang up in America around the turn of the century. One poll acclaimed her America's "most useful citizen," and all polls listed her among the nation's most famous women. She lost some of her popularity and much of her financial backing when she took a strong public stand against World War I. As a committed pacifist, she had no choice; to her, work for peace was as important as the work on Halsted Street.

Years after the war, her pacifist stance was rewarded when she was given the 1931 Nobel Peace Prize. She was the first American woman to be honored with a Nobel Prize. By that time, her popularity was fully restored, and a poll proclaimed her "the world's greatest woman." In 1934 she was celebrated at a banquet for 1,200 people in the nation's capital. After listening patiently to all the speeches of the evening giving testimony to her and to her work, 74-year-old Jane Addams rose from her place of honor and said simply: "I do not know any such person as you have described here tonight."

In a sense Jane Addams was right. She did not consider her work finished, for she had certainly not accomplished all that she had wanted to do through Hull House. Right in her own neighborhood people still lived in poverty, children still suffered and still got into trouble, streets were still littered, housing and schools were still inadequate. Nonetheless, when anything went wrong on the West Side of Chicago, when anyone had troubles too great to bear, the natural place to go was Hull House.* Jane Addams had made a definite impact on her world. But she had done more than take care of one neighborhood. She had changed a nation's way of looking at its poor and its strangers. That was what the 1,200 people had gathered in Washington, D.C., to celebrate, and that was Jane Addams's greatest contribution to her country. At her death from cancer in 1935, her body lay in state at Hull House for two days while her friends and neighbors filed past in mourning and in tribute. "Her heart was alive to the wants of the poor," said her eulogist. "If you would see her monument, look around you."

---

* Hull House remained the center of its neighborhood until 1963 when it was razed; the property became a part of the Chicago campus of the University of Illinois.

2

She Dared to Make
the Stone Flat

"*As I fall on my knees, with my face to the rising sun, oh, Lord, have mercy on me . . . .*" *As the eight-year-old sang the spiritual, she felt her heart would burst with the power of the words and the music. She could feel the afternoon sun streaming in through the stained glass windows in a warm rainbow of light that felt like the rainbow of song she was making. As the last notes faded, the congregation remained silent, as if breathing too loudly would break the spell.*

It was Mr. Robinson, the director, who brought them all back. "Amen," he said softly, turning to face the audience. Then louder, "I say 'Amen,' people." And a shower of "Amens" answered him. "The Lord has given this young lady a mighty gift," he began, "the gift of song. And she has used that gift to touch our hearts today. Bless you, child," he said, turning back to Marian, "and to God be the glory."

16

"*You're mighty quiet for a big-time singer,*" *her father teased as they walked home together.* "*I thought you'd be excited.*"

Marian just smiled and squeezed his hand a little tighter. She was excited, but not jump-up-and-down excited. It was more like be-quiet-and-remember excited, for she was lost in the memory of the sound that had flowed out from her and floated over the people of Union Baptist Church. She was sorry it was all over. Now there was nothing to look forward to.

As they turned down their own street, Marian saw her mother out front with her two little sisters. She broke into a run. "*Oh, Mama, it was wonderful!*"

"*I know, dear, I know all about it,*" *her mother said as she gave her a big hug.*

"*But how could you know already?*" *Marian asked, pulling back in surprise.*

"*Because Mr. Robinson himself rode by here just after the service—to ask you to sing again next Sunday!*"

"*Oh, Mama!*" *Marian said, grabbing up baby Ethel and swinging her around.* "*Maybe next time you can all go!*"

"*Hold on there,*" *said her father.* "*I'm not going to have them singing my child to death.*"

"*Nonsense,*" *laughed her mother.* "*They'd have to do some singing to sing that child to death. That girl just plain loves to sing.*"

Marian smiled. Yes, they'd have to do some singing to wear her down, for if she had to think about it, she guessed she really did just plain love to sing. And her love of singing changed our world. Not only did Marian Anderson *develop her voice into one of the finest contraltos* ever heard, but she broke through the ugly barriers of race that had previously kept blacks from the stages of America's concert halls and opera houses.*

G rowing up in a mixed neighborhood in South Philadelphia, Marian Anderson did not know until her teen years the handicap her race imposed on her. She was born on February 17, 1902, the first of John and Annie Anderson's three daughters. Though the family was poor, it was close and loving, and Marian Anderson never thought of herself as "deprived." Though there were certainly many things she never had, she never missed them, because, as she later put it, she had "the things that mattered."

Among the things Marian Anderson never had as a young child were professional lessons, for though her family was aware that she had a special talent, they could not afford the voice training they knew she should have. But from the age of six, Marian Anderson sang in the choir at the Union Baptist Church. That in its own way provided invaluable training, for it not only introduced her to the deep spirituality of music but it also gave her the ability to sing with ease in front of large audiences. In addition, weekly practices and Sunday performances of the Union Baptist choir provided a unique opportunity for the development of Marian Anderson's magnificent range. Week after week

---

* A contralto is the lowest range of the female voice.

she took home the music and practiced all the parts. Come Sunday, should any soloist, whether soprano, alto, tenor, or bass, be absent, young Marian was ready to fill in. Hers was a genius that was not to be denied.

It was a genius of which her father, John Anderson, was justly proud. A tall, handsome, hardworking man, Anderson encouraged her in her singing, and his sudden death when she was nine left her with many loving memories. Upon the death of her father, Marian, her sisters, and her mother moved in with his parents. Her mother, who had been a teacher in her native Virginia, supported the family as a cleaning woman and a laundress, while her grandmother looked after the girls at home.

It was her mother's quiet strength and deep faith that were to be the abiding influences in Marian Anderson's life. As she grew older and came to realize that the only limit to her success was the color of her skin, the reserve from which she drew her unfailing calm was the rich heritage of her mother, who taught her that bitterness and anger were not appropriate weapons with which to fight prejudice. By her example she taught, as well, the quiet power of believing, simply believing that right would be done, that when one way was barred another would be found. "We grew up in this atmosphere of faith she created," Marian Anderson later recalled, "aware that Mother had strength beyond the energies of her small body."

Mrs. Anderson also taught Marian and her sisters the importance of hard work in achieving goals. Even as a young girl, Marian added to the family income by scrubbing porch steps, a job she undertook with the same intensity and thoroughness she was afterward to give to her professional training. That training began when she was still in high school. A neighbor, whose voice Marian greatly admired, gave her free lessons. Encouraged, she decided to enroll in a Philadelphia music school. It was at that point that Marian Anderson first met the cruelty of prejudice. She was more shocked than humiliated when she was dismissed with a single sentence: "We don't take colored."

Though her mother assured her there would be "another way," Marian had all but decided that as a black singer she could never expect to achieve her goals when she was invited to sing on the same program as Roland Hayes. Hayes, a tenor, was the first black American to sing classical music professionally, and Marian realized that if Hayes had found a way to obtain the proper training, then perhaps she could find one, too.

As she said years later, "My mother taught me you can't do anything by yourself. There's always somebody to make the stone flat for you to stand on." This time it was the black community of Philadelphia, people who had heard her sing in their churches, who made the stone flat by starting "The Fund for Marian's Future," a fund that gave her a year's lessons with Agnes Reifsnyder, the most famous contralto in the area. At the end of that time, Anderson's friends helped her schedule a concert, and the proceeds from that event enabled her to begin lessons with Giuseppe Boghetti, who was to remain her teacher for years thereafter.

Boghetti was a demanding teacher, explaining that there was no shortcut to becoming a real professional, for "only when you understand the how and why of singing will you be able to perform well. . . ." Sometimes he and Marian acted out entire scenes from operas, but when she confided to him that she enjoyed acting and might like to try opera, Boghetti said, "For you, the concert stage is better." His advice made her realize that not even Roland Hayes had ever sung with a major American opera company.

Setting such dreams aside, she turned her attention to the concert stage, embarking on her first tour at age 19. Traveling through the South and singing at black colleges, she experienced segregation first hand. She was forced to sleep sitting up in the parlor cars of trains and to stay with black families who opened their homes to her rather than in hotels whose doors were closed to blacks. But this tour, while awakening her to the reality of Jim Crow laws*, also provided her with one exhilarating moment that evoked the memory of her first performance as a child and foretold the excitement that was to come. At a performance at Howard University in Washington, D.C., in the middle of singing one of Richard Strauss's works, she had the overwhelming sensation that " 'Morgen' seemed mine to do with as I pleased. There are such moments in a career," she wrote later, "when you feel that you belong to a thing and it belongs to you . . . I was certain then . . . I would be able to do whatever I undertook."

Such confidence was a bit premature. Coming home from her well-received tour of the South, she accepted an engagement in New York City's Town Hall. Her career had advanced to a level that seemed to call for exposure to a

---

* "Jim Crow laws" were laws that prohibited blacks from entering certain public areas, that is, most hotels and restaurants, and assigned them to inferior sections in theaters, trains, and streetcars.

larger audience, and Town Hall represented the main-
stream of American musical life. But she was just 20 years
old and had as yet neither the experience nor the training
to attempt such a performance. The recital was coolly
received by a small audience, and the New York City
music critics were not kind in their reviews.

Marian Anderson was crushed. She returned home to
Philadelphia, withdrew from her lessons, and brooded for
months in her studio. She considered giving up music and
going into medicine, a course she had pondered several
times before. But gradually her mother's gentle persuasion
revived her confidence and enthusiasm, and she returned to
her lessons.

Years of hard work followed. She sang American spirit-
uals with command and color, for she was singing in her own
language the songs she had heard all her life. But the great
arias and lieders are written and performed in the European languages, and Marian Anderson knew that the critics
were right—to sing them well, one had to know the languages in which they were written. She could not feel
what she did not fully understand, and she could not really
sing what she did not feel. Determined to make the music
of the ages her own, she took up the serious study of Italian,
French, and German.

In 1925 she entered and won a contest to sing with the
New York Philharmonic Orchestra. That performance was
given before thousands of people in Lewisohn Stadium. "A
remarkable voice was heard last night," one critic wrote.
It was a voice of velvet, a voice of a hundred different
colors, and of an absolutely amazing range. Anderson appeared that same year in Carnegie Hall to the same critical

raves. A career of great promise seemed open to her. But over the next few years, she found it harder and harder to book engagements in the concert halls of major American cities. Because Marian Anderson was black, there was no stage for her in her own country.

Like many black performers before her, Anderson decided to go to Europe to study and sing there. In 1930, she made the first of several tours of Europe. She sang for Jean Sibelius, the great composer, at his home in Finland. Sibelius, then almost 70, was moved. "Miss Anderson, my roof is too low for you," he said as he embraced her. In Austria she performed before an audience that included Arturo Toscanini, the famous Italian conductor. "Yours is a voice such as one hears once in a hundred years," he told her backstage. She was to have sung next in concert in Berlin, but the performance was cancelled when Adolf Hitler, newly appointed Chancellor of Germany, discovered that she was black.

Over the next five years Marian Anderson studied in Europe and sang before the kings and queens of Sweden, Norway, Denmark, and England. Yet she was still relatively unknown in the United States. Then she was "discovered" in Paris by Sol Hurok, the flamboyant American concert manager. Hurok convinced her that with the proper management she could have a successful career in America, and Marian Anderson was ready to try. "I wanted to come home," she wrote. "I had to test myself as a serious artist in my own country." In 1935, at the peak of her fame in Europe, she set sail for the United States.

With her was Kosti Vehanen, the Scandinavian accompanist who had been at her side through five years of

European concerts. Hurok had warned her that there might be trouble in America if she appeared on stage with a white accompanist, but she knew Vehanen's sound musicianship was essential to her continued development and decided to take the risk.

Their first concert back home was scheduled for New York City's Town Hall, and Marian Anderson was determined to be at her best for this return to the hall where she had suffered her most dismal failure. But during rough seas on the ocean voyage home, she slipped, breaking her ankle. Undaunted, she kept her date at Town Hall, using the curtain to mask her awkward entrance and exit and leaning against the piano as she sang. Her performance was widely acclaimed, and all the painful memories of her earlier appearance on that stage were erased. "Let it be said at the outset," proclaimed the *New York Times*'s music critic, "Marian Anderson has returned to her native land one of the great singers of our times." She sang again in Carnegie Hall, and she sang in the White House for President and Mrs. Franklin Roosevelt. She made a tour of the United States, singing before sell-out crowds in over 70 cities across the country. It seemed that she had finally established herself as a premier American artist. The fact that she was black seemed no longer a handicap.

But in 1939 the Daughters of the American Revolution cancelled a Marian Anderson concert scheduled for Constitution Hall in Washington, D.C., explaining that their hall "could not be used by one of [her] race." Anderson accepted this affront as she had accepted all the bigotry she'd faced before, with philosophic patience. She did not need Constitution Hall. She had other stages for her talent.

There was, as her mother had said, "another way." But other Americans rose to her defense. Eleanor Roosevelt resigned her membership in the DAR and persuaded Harold Ickes, the Secretary of the Interior, to offer Marian Anderson the use of the Lincoln Memorial for an outdoor concert.

There, on Easter Sunday, a crowd of 75,000 assembled to hear her. "Genius, like justice, is blind," Ickes said in introducing her. "Genius draws no color line." It was an emotional event for both the performer and her audience. "I had a sensation unlike any I had experienced before," she said. "I wondered whether I would be able to sing." She was, of course, more than able to sing. She opened the concert, which was broadcast all over the country, with the national anthem, then continued through a program that included "America" and Schubert's "Ave Maria." It was a performance that engraved itself on the nation's conscience.

America had finally given her its undivided attention and affection. And not without cause. The woman they honored was a vocal genius. She never performed music in the traditional way, but made each song her own. Whether she sang Brahms, Schubert, Handel, Strauss, Debussy, or an American spiritual, she infused each song with beauty and drama from within. A tall, slender woman in her youth, statuesque in maturity, she had a physical strength that lent power to her voice.

In 1943 Marian Anderson married Orpheus "King" Fisher, a well-established architect she had met early in her career. When she was not on tour, the couple lived quietly near Danbury, Connecticut, on a small farm they called Marianna. There Anderson practiced long hours in a studio her husband had built for her. With the end of World War II, she resumed her world tours. Before her career ended she had sung in Europe, South America, Africa, and the Far East. Truly an international artist, she was called the world's greatest contralto and seemed to have reached all her goals.

But one remained. In January of 1955, she made another major breakthrough by appearing with the New York Metropolitan Opera Company, the first black to sing with the company. "For you, the concert stage is better," Boghetti had advised many years earlier. But as she walked on stage that night, before she even began to sing her role as Ulrica in Verdi's *The Masked Ball*, the audience rose to give her a standing ovation. Though she had broken the last major racial barrier on the American musical stage, the triumph came too late in her career for her to turn seriously to opera. She was 53, well past the age when singers normally make their operatic debuts, and she acknowledged, "I wish it had come earlier that I might have been able to bring more to it."

Marian Anderson brought all she could to everything she did. A reserved and private person of a very generous nature, she challenged and broke racial barriers quietly, with dignity and without fanfare. She received her many honors graciously. In 1941 she received the Bok Award given to the outstanding citizen of Philadelphia. The city of her birth also built a modern recreation center in her old neighborhood and named it in her honor. In 1958, President Eisenhower appointed her a United States delegate to the United Nations. In 1961, she sang the national anthem at the inauguration of John F. Kennedy. And two

Marian Anderson at the beginning of her career

Marian Anderson at 75

years later the Presidential Medal of Freedom, the nation's highest civilian award, was bestowed on her by Lyndon Johnson.

In 1964 she made her farewell tour of the nation, and a year later, at age 63, she retired. She has lived ever since in Danbury with her husband of 40 years, enjoying such hobbies as upholstering and photography and giving much of her time to the administration of a scholarship fund she established for the benefit of worthy young musicians of all races, her way of making the stone flat for others to stand on.

Though her public appearances have been rare since her retirement, on July 4, 1976, at the nation's bicentennial fete, Marian Anderson read the Declaration of Independence. And in February of 1977 she attended a benefit performance at Carnegie Hall on the occasion of her seventy-fifth birthday. Before the great figures of American music who gathered to honor her, Rosalynn Carter, the First Lady, read a congressional resolution commending her for her "untiring and unselfish devotion to the promotion of the arts in this country."

The legacy of Marian Anderson lies not only in the magnificence of her voice, which we can still hear in recordings of the songs that have become so closely associated with her—"America," "Summertime," "He's Got the Whole World in His Hands"—it lies as well in the significance of her achievements in a field that had been closed to blacks.

Those achievements were properly and dramatically acknowledged at an eightieth birthday celebration at Carnegie Hall in February of 1982. Shirley Verrett and Grace

Brumbry, two black sopranos who began their operatic careers after winning Marian Anderson scholarships, honored the legendary contralto with a concert. "She was," said Verrett on the night of the performance, "a dream-maker, giving us the right to dream the undreamable, reach for the unreachable, and achieve the impossible. Her courage has indeed changed the course of history, and she has cast a shadow that embraces us all."

3

She Dared to Defend the Web of Life

"*Charlotte! Come here!*"

"*What is it?*" *the girl asked as she fell to her hands and knees at the grassy edge of the pond.*

"*Got him!*" *said Rachel, triumphantly scooping up a dripping jarful of muddy water.*

"*What is it?*"

"*I don't know,*" *Rachel said, shaking the jar so that the water swirled 'round and 'round, then abruptly tilting it so that the water pooled to one side.* "*There! Just look at him!*" *she said, shoving the jar under her friend's nose.*

"*Look at what? All I see is a moldy old twig.*"

"*Keep looking,*" *Rachel urged.* "*It's alive.*"

"*Oh, it's moving. And something's coming out of one end. It looks like an ant. What is it, Rachel?*"

"*I don't know, but I'll bet we can find it in the field book.*"

The two girls scrambled to their feet and started home across the woods, eager to compare the creature in the jar to the pictures in the insect book. But before they reached the back yard, they heard Rachel's mother calling.

"Coming, Mom," Rachel sang out. "And I've got something to show you." As she walked through the trees and into the open, she could see that her mother was holding up a magazine.

"It's the St. Nicholas!" Rachel shouted, breaking into a run. "Maybe they've published my story!"

"Here, here," her mother laughed, holding the magazine just out of reach. "First tell me what's in the jar."

"Oh, Mother," Rachel pleaded, setting the jar on the porch rail. "That can wait. Let me see it, please!"

As her mother handed her the magazine, Rachel plopped down on the steps, squeezed her eyes shut, and took a deep breath. Then she flipped back the cover and ran her finger quickly down the table of contents. There it was—"A Battle in the Clouds," Silver Badge winner for September 1918.

"Oh, Rachel," Charlotte exclaimed, giving her a hug. "I just knew you could do it! You're the best writer in the whole school, and everybody knows it, too."

"It's nothing, really," came the quiet reply. But deep inside, ten-year-old Rachel Carson knew that having her article published in St. Nicholas magazine was far from nothing. It was, in fact, everything, for she knew that when she grew up she would be a writer, and winning the Silver Badge was her first real step toward that all-important goal. What she did not know yet, what she had no way of knowing, was that her fascination with insects, birds, and other animals, her sense of wonder at the complex world of nature, would lead her to become an accomplished scien-

*tist who would use the written word to teach her readers
the meaning of the word "ecology" and to urge them to do
all within their power to protect the web of life that modern chemicals threatened to destroy.*

Born May 27, 1907, in Springdale, Pennsylvania, Rachel
Louise Carson grew up along the Allegheny River,
with her father's 65 acres of woodland as her playground.
Robert Warden Carson dabbled in real estate and had
bought the land hoping to sell it at a profit, but he ended
up keeping it through the growing-up years of his children.
His wife, Maria McLean Carson, loved the birds and animals who lived on the wooded acres and passed along that
love to her oldest children, then to Rachel, born when
Marian was ten and Robert eight.

Life was so sacred to Mrs. Carson that she never killed
flies or spiders but merely caught them and set them free
outdoors. In addition to a reverence for life, young Rachel
learned from her parents a love of music and books. Her
father had been a member of a traveling church quartet
when he met her mother, and the family spent many evenings harmonizing around the fireplace. They spent time
with books, too, and by the time Rachel was eight she was
making books of her own, including one with pictures and
rhymes made especially for her father.

Her quiet world of books and fields was disturbed when
the United States entered World War I and her brother
Robert went into training as a pilot. His letters home inspired the story that brought ten-year-old Rachel her first
publication in *St. Nicholas*. Within a year there were two

more, one of which earned her the magazine's Gold Badge. Her interest in writing continued through her high school years.

Upon graduation, Rachel chose Pennsylvania College for Women, later called Chatham College, because it was small, fairly close to home, and had high academic standards. It was also expensive, and although she earned a small scholarship, she had to borrow money to put herself through school. She had little to spend on trips to town, and she seldom went places with her classmates, preferring to spend her time in the library studying. She maintained her close family ties, going home as often as possible and inviting her mother up for those weekends when she needed to stay on campus. As a freshman, she still believed she would become a writer and chose literature as her major. She was a reporter for the college newspaper, and her stories were published in the school's literary magazine. One of those stories was about a cat's right to be "independent and as good as anyone else." That cat could have been Rachel herself, going her own way among classmates who respected her but never really grew close to her.

Her second year at Chatham brought new direction to her life. A biology class taught by Mary Skinker revived her interest in science. She developed a deep friendship with young Skinker and changed her major, in spite of the fact that her professors warned her that it was a mistake for a woman to give up a promising career in writing to try to enter the man's world of science. But there was no turning back. Suddenly Rachel Carson knew that work in the real world of nature was more important to her than work in make-believe worlds. Though she did not realize it at the time, changing majors did not mean that she was to abandon writing. It simply meant that now she would have something to write about, something more important to her than anything else in the world.

After Rachel graduated with honors in 1929, it was Mary Skinker who helped her get a summer fellowship at the U.S. Marine Biology Laboratory at Cape Cod, Massachusetts, and a one-year fellowship for graduate work at Johns Hopkins University in Baltimore, Maryland. It was at Cape Cod that Rachel Carson first experienced the sea. She had read and written of the ocean since childhood, but now she smelled it and heard it and saw it for herself. She was never to forget that experience, nor ever again to stay away from the ocean for any length of time.

For six weeks she worked in the field, gathering specimens from the sea, and then spent the next six weeks in the laboratory, bending over a microscope for long hours, examining the specimens she had found during her field work. She thought that once she finished her graduate work she would like to work for the U.S. Bureau of Fisheries. But when she approached the supervisor, Elmer Higgins, he discouraged her, telling her that there wasn't much a "lady biologist" could do except teach in a high school or college.

Ignoring his advice, Rachel began a year of graduate school at Johns Hopkins. Realizing that her research would take far longer than her one-year fellowship could pay for, she took a job as a laboratory assistant at Johns Hopkins and persuaded her father to move the family to Baltimore. Over the next few years she became a half-time assistant in zoology at the University of Maryland and taught summer sessions at Johns Hopkins, all the while working toward her master's degree in marine biology. She received that degree in 1932 and continued her part-time teaching.

Her father's death in 1935 meant that she needed steady work in order to help support her mother and herself. She went back to Elmer Higgins of the U.S. Bureau of Fisheries; this time he told her he might have work for her—if she could write. He needed a series of seven-minute radio spots on marine life, and his other assistants were having trouble turning scientific language into programs ordinary radio listeners could understand and enjoy. Her sample radio spots were so lively that he offered her a half-time position. At the end of the year Rachel, the only woman to take the Civil Service exam for a position on Higgins's staff, made the highest score and was offered a full-time job as an aquatic biologist.

At this point, she and her mother decided to move from Baltimore to Silver Spring, Maryland, so that she could be closer to the Fisheries Lab where she worked. Within a year life changed drastically for mother and daughter. Marian, Rachel's sister, died and left two grade-school daughters, Marjorie and Virginia. Mrs. Carson felt they should take the girls, and suddenly Rachel found herself responsible for the support of a small family.

She worked hard at her job with the Fisheries Lab, writing a series of pamphlets on sea creatures. When Elmer Higgins decided the pamphlets should be put into a booklet for Fisheries personnel, he asked Rachel to write an introduction for the series. Her introduction, full of her excitement over the mysteries of the sea, was beautiful and inspiring, but it was hardly an appropriate introduction to a scientific treatise on the creatures of the ocean. And Elmer Higgins told her so. "You've written this on Fisheries Lab time," he said, "but we can't use it. Write something we can use on your own time, then send this in to the *Atlantic*." Rachel took his advice, and in September of 1937, nearly 20 years after her first essay had appeared in *St. Nicholas*, the prestigious *Atlantic Monthly* published "Undersea."

The event was a turning point in Rachel Carson's life. Caught up in graduate school research and technical writing for the Fisheries Lab and aware that the family depended upon her for their living, she had all but given up her dream of becoming a writer. Now letters from readers of the *Atlantic Monthly* article made her feel that there were people who wanted to read more of her work.

Mr. Higgins agreed. He urged her to write a book about the world under the sea. But when would she write it? She had received only $75 for the *Atlantic Monthly* article; she could hardly afford to quit her job and become a full-time writer. Still, when a book publisher from New York said he was interested in seeing some of her work, the old dreams came rushing back, and she told him she'd find the time— somehow. She found it by working late into the night, her cat Mitzi often sleeping at her feet as she typed page after page. Three years later, in November of 1941, *Under the Sea-Wind* was published. It was dedicated to her mother, the woman who had taught her a love of nature, but she added a special inscription to the copy she took to Elmer Higgins: "To Mr. Higgins who started it all."

The hard work was over. The book was out. But by December 7, less than a month after publication, readers who might have spent pleasant hours reading about Scomber the mackerel, Anguilla the eel, and Rynchops the black skimmer were suddenly reading about other sea adventures. Pearl Harbor had been attacked by the Japanese, and America was involved in World War II. In 1942 Rachel's department, now the Fish and Wildlife Service, was moved to Chicago, Illinois. Rachel, her mother, and her two nieces moved too, spending a little over a year in nearby Evanston before returning to their home in Silver Spring.

By 1946 Rachel Carson was assistant to the chief of the Office of Information of the Fish and Wildlife Service, and by 1949 she was editor-in-chief of the information division. In between her pressing editorial duties, she began moving toward a new book. This time she wanted an agent to handle her business dealings with publishers, and she found Mary Rodell. Within a year Rodell had landed a contract for a new Rachel Carson book with Oxford University Press, and Rachel began work in earnest. She and her agent took several trips together in search of material for the new book. They spent a week on *Albatross III*, the Fish and Wildlife survey ship, the first women to be asked aboard. In the laboratory below deck Carson joined biologists who studied sea creatures captured by the ship's crew, and in the wheelhouse she listened in fascination to speakers hooked to hydrophones that brought them the secret sounds of the world beneath the waters.

But Rachel decided that if she wanted to write about life beneath the waters, she herself had to go under the sea. She donned a diving helmet and renewed her work in the waters off the coast of Florida. Though she found the sound of air hissing into the helmet "annoying" and though she did not enjoy the sensation of lead weights on her feet, she felt the experience taught her much about the world she was trying to capture and was well worth the small discomfort it cost her. By now she had most of the material, but she needed time if she was to complete her work by the deadline called for in her contract. A fellowship, awarded her in August of 1949, gave her that time by providing enough money for her to take a year's leave without pay from her government job.

It was a new experience, a new world, for Rachel Carson. She was able to keep her own hours, working well into the night, sleeping in, then working again until she felt too tired to go on. She felt free, and she knew that if she could ever afford to do so, she would like to spend the rest of her life writing in this way. Her mother, though now 81 years old, was fully involved in the work, and it was she who typed the final draft of Rachel's second book, even as she had typed *Under the Sea-Wind*. In July of 1950 the job was done—*The Sea Around Us* was about to become a reality.

This time there was no war to distract the American public from Rachel Carson's work, and the honors came quickly. The book won a $1,000 prize from the American Association for the Advancement of Science, the John Burroughs Medal for natural history, and the National Book Award. For 81 weeks *The Sea Around Us* was on best-seller lists, and Rachel Carson became an important figure on the literary scene.

She was a strange figure, for she wrote not of make-believe worlds but of real ones, and readers by the thousands wanted to read more and more about those worlds. By combining a scholar's knowledge of science with a poet's talent for words, she taught the American public to look at nature in a new way. Readers clamored for more, and, to her surprise, they wanted to meet the woman who had given them those new worlds. Suddenly this very private person became a celebrity. Though she was terrified of crowds, she didn't show her fear, and her audiences responded warmly. Time after time she made public appearances, though she confessed to a friend, "The truth is I'm much more at home barefoot in the sand or on shipboard in sneakers than on hardwood floors in high heels."

Fan mail poured in, including letters from aspiring young writers who admired her work. Remembering her childhood dreams, she encouraged beginners to keep trying, confessing that she herself had received countless rejection slips for her poetry and short stories and explaining that "Given the initial talent . . . writing is largely a matter of application and hard work, of writing and rewriting endlessly. . . ." And when young writers asked what they should write about, she answered, "If you write what you yourself sincerely think and feel and are interested in, the chances are very high that you will interest other people as well."

With fame came other offers. In 1953 *The Sea Around Us* was made into a movie. Though the picture won an Oscar for the best feature-length documentary, Rachel Carson found it a disappointment and was not interested in seeing any of her other works made into movies.

Movie rights, along with Book-of-the-Month Club sales, meant that Rachel Carson had money to build a summer house on the coast of Maine, and in 1952 she and her mother picked out 1½ acres on the west shore of Boothbay Harbor and built a small home there. Over the years that summer home became the one place where the busy writer could find peace and the inspiration to carry on her work.

The work was pressing now, for although she had been awarded a 1951 Guggenheim Fellowship for work on a third book, she was finding it hard to work, caught up as she was in the success of *The Sea Around Us*. Honorary doctorates from Chatham College, her alma mater, and from other colleges across the country were awarded her, and she was made a Fellow of the Royal Society of Literature in England. With all the travel, she continued to work on her new book, and in March of 1953 wrote that she was far behind schedule but "at least I am in that state of desperate determination that—judging by the past—is likely to bring me through about on time." She did come through on time, and in 1955 *The Edge of the Sea* appeared.

This time Rachel Carson was writing about the seashore, the land area surrounding the sea. Hardly was the new book completed before more honors and new offers began pouring in. The book won the achievement award of the American Association of University Women, and Rachel Carson spoke to that group in 1955, echoing thoughts she had expressed some years earlier in a letter to a young writer:

> Writing is a lonely occupation at best. Of course there are stimulating and even happy associations with friends and colleagues, but during the actual work of creation the writer cuts himself off from all others and confronts his

subject alone. He moves into a realm where he has never been before—perhaps where no one has ever been. It is a lonely place, and even a little frightening. . . .

Frightening or not, writing was the task she had given her life to, and she told her audience that she was already at work on something new, since "No writer can stand still. He continues to create or he perishes. Each task completed carries its own obligation to go on to something new."

Actually, she was at work on several new things. She wrote a script for a television special on clouds and wrote "Help Your Child to Wonder," a magazine article inspired by her trips to the seashore with her great-nephew Roger. The article became a book, *A Sense of Wonder*, a year later. In 1957, just a few months after that article appeared, Roger's mother Marjorie died and Rachel Carson, now 50 years old, adopted the ten-year-old boy. Once more, she was in charge of a family. But the family grew smaller the very next year when Mrs. Carson died, and Roger and Rachel were left alone in the house in Silver Spring.

That year was a crucial one for Rachel, for she had begun to look in a new direction, a direction that was to lead her to the book for which she is best remembered. As she had once told a reporter, "I am always more interested in what I am about to do than in what I have already done," and what she was about to do was different from anything she had yet done. In January of 1958 a long-time friend sent Rachel a copy of a letter describing what happened when an airplane pilot sprayed the woods near her house with DDT, an insecticide used to combat mosquitoes. The story was not a pleasant one:

The "harmless" shower bath killed seven of our lovely
song-birds outright. We picked up three dead bodies the
next morning. . . . the next day three were scattered around
the bird bath. I had emptied it and scrubbed it after the
spraying, but YOU CAN NEVER KILL DDT.

YOU CAN NEVER KILL DDT. Those words rang in Rachel
Carson's ears, for she knew that her friend was right. All
over America people were spraying their crops and trees
and rivers with chemicals intended to kill pests. But did the
killing stop there? Could chemicals that stayed in the food
chain destroy fish, birds, and animals farther up the chain?
Were humans themselves being endangered by the widespread use of such chemicals? The more she read about
the subject, the more she became convinced that she must
write about dangers that no one else was pointing out.

But should she try it? She had been riding a wave of
success, and now she was considering risking everything
on this very different book. It was a risk she had to take,
for, as she wrote a friend, ". . . knowing what I do, I have
no choice but to set it down to be read by those who will."
Setting it down would be no easy task. She hired an assistant
to serve as secretary and researcher, knowing that she had
to make every effort to back up her words with scientific
proof, since her work was bound to be attacked by the
powerful companies who manufactured the various chemicals used on gardens, fields, and forests. She could not even
be sure how the government would react to what she had to
say, since the U.S. Department of Agriculture recommended the use of herbicides and pesticides as the best way

to get maximum yields from America's farms. Nonetheless, she knew this story had to be told.

Long years of research, writing, and rewriting went into the telling. The story, when it was finished, opened with a description of the natural beauty of a fictitious town before a white powder was sprayed from the sky, before the "shadow of death" fell upon the town and "only silence lay over the fields and wood and marsh." And she called the book *Silent Spring*, words that expressed her message simply but powerfully.

Carson's message—that the destruction of any part of the web of life threatened all else within that web, including the human race itself—was a brave and frightening statement, a far cry from her gentle books on sea and shore. Would America listen? The attacks began even before the book itself was released, for on June 16, 1962, *The New Yorker* magazine published the first part of a condensed version of *Silent Spring*. There was immediate and angry response. Rachel Carson was accused of being a sentimental birdwatcher who would rather see people starve when their crops were destroyed by insects than see one robin die from DDT. But mixed with the accusations were honors. She won the Schweitzer Medal of the Animal Welfare Institute, the Conservationist of the Year Award from the National Wildlife Federation, and the American Geographical Society Award. She also became the first woman to receive the Audubon Society's medal for achievement in conservation and one of only three women to be elected to the 50-member American Academy of Arts and Letters.

In addition, she was flooded with letters of appreciation

Rachel Carson at 10

Rachel Carson shortly after the publication of *Silent Spring*

from thousands of readers who had never before stopped to think that many of the chemicals being sprayed into the air poisoned the soil and water onto which they fell. Before *Silent Spring*, these people had had no idea that when elms were sprayed with DDT, the chemical seeped into the soil and was eaten by earthworms. Though the worms seemed unharmed by the DDT, robins who ate them died. And the pattern continued for years after each spraying. How far up the food chain were such poisons traveling?

And DDT was not the only culprit. In the years after World War II, chemists had developed a long list of pesticides they claimed would destroy harmful insects. Rachel Carson told the other side of the story, warning that those insects who survived the chemical sprays would eventually breed young who were immune to the sprays. There were better ways of fighting insects, ways that did not poison the air, water, and soil. She urged the use of biological controls that were "based on understanding of the living organisms they seek to control [and of] the whole fabric of life to which those organisms belong."

Although her critics tried to prove her wrong, they could not. Within a year, the United States government issued a report that not only confirmed her warning that pesticides were silencing the song of life but cited her book as the only available reliable source of information on the subject. The facts were solid. The battle was won. But the war against poisoning our universe was far from over. What would people do, now that they knew the dangers? Rachel Carson's *Silent Spring* had attacked a long-standing belief that harm to nature was the inevitable price of progress. Her discussions of biological control of insects suggested that progress need not mean the destruction of our environment, and her book did much to launch the environmental movement that swept America over the next decade.

Rachel Carson did not live to see the changes that movement brought about. A breast tumor removed in 1960 proved to be cancerous, and her work on *Silent Spring* had been carried out amid many tests and treatments, none of which stopped the spread of the deadly disease. She wrote to a friend, "I keep thinking—if only I could have reached this point ten years ago! Now when there is an opportunity to do so much, my body falters and I know there is little time left."

Time ran out for Rachel Carson on April 14, 1964, but not before she had alerted the world to the dangers of polluting its air, water, and soil. In 1980 President Jimmy Carter posthumously awarded this courageous author the Presidential Medal of Freedom, the government's highest civilian award. But there are other tributes that would mean even more to Rachel Carson. There are the songs of robins on a spring morning, the hum of bees in a field of wild flowers, sounds that we are still able to enjoy because one woman used her talents as poet and scientist to give the world an urgent message it did not really want to hear.

4

She Dared to Challenge the Dangerous Trades

"*I liked her,*" *insisted 11-year-old Alice.* "*Sometimes she was scary looking, but I liked what she said about helping those children whose father was always drinking.*"

"*Mrs. Willard could tell you lots more stories like that,*" *said her mother.* "*Frances Willard knows more about the down-and-out people of this country than most of us ever will.*"

"*Friend of the poor but enemy of Bacchus,*" *said Alice's father, lifting his wine glass and giving her mother a knowing look.* "*She wouldn't have been very welcome at the feast of Dionysus.*"

"*Who was Dionysus?*" *asked Alice.*

"*And Bacchus?*" *asked nine-year-old Margaret.*

"*Dionysus was the Greek god of wine,*" *said Edith, the oldest of the sisters.* "*He was also called Bacchus. He's in* Bullfinch's Mythology."

"*I wonder if Bullfinch tells whether Greek fathers ever got drunk and beat their wives and children,*" *said Alice,*

47

*still lost in her memories of Frances Willard's stories of the
drunkards of Chicago's slums.*

*"Not likely," said her mother. "Men didn't tend to write
about women and children."*

*"Mrs. Willard says most people don't even care about
women and children," said Alice, "or about anybody who's
poor."*

"Mrs. Willard believes in her cause," said her father.

*"And Grandma believes in it, too," said Alice. "She gave
her some money."*

*"I don't doubt it," said her father. "Your grandmother
would give away her last penny."*

*"You mean she might run out?" asked little Nora, sud-
denly alarmed.*

*"No, she'll not likely run out," her father chuckled.
"Your grandfather left her enough to share."*

*"She earned every penny of it," said her mother. "She
gave him the best years of her life and bore him 11 children.
You have no idea what it is to give up your freedom to a
man. Grandmother Hamilton was an old woman before
she had a life of her own."*

*Alice squirmed uncomfortably. Her mother's favorite
subject was freedom. She had told them over and over
again that personal liberty was the most precious thing in
life. But if Grandmother Hamilton hadn't given up some
of her freedom to marry, then she wouldn't have had
enough money to help the poor. She sighed and looked
down at the food on her plate. She had roast and potatoes
and peas, but in the slums of Chicago there were people
who had no dinner at all. She stabbed angrily at her peas.
When she grew up she'd find a way to make things better*

for those people—and she'd do it without giving up one bit of her personal liberty!

Alice Hamilton managed to do just that, becoming the founder of industrial medicine in the United States and enjoying a career that gave her the freedom to earn her own way in the world and the opportunity to serve others as she went along.

Born on February 27, 1869, while her mother was visiting relatives in New York City, Alice Hamilton spent her growing-up years in Ft. Wayne, Indiana, on the estate where Grandfather Hamilton had first built a home years before and where three of his children had established their own homes. He died before Alice was born, but Grandmother Emerine Holman Hamilton was a primary influence in Alice's early life. Grandmother Hamilton's interest in temperance and suffrage led her to invite workers in both fields to the family estate, and Alice and her three sisters, along with other Hamilton grandchildren, were often introduced to guests such as Frances Willard and allowed to listen to their talk on reform.*

Alice's mother, Gertrude Pond Hamilton, enjoyed meeting people who were doing their part to change things. She

---

* Temperance and suffrage were two reform movements of the late nineteenth and early twentieth centuries. The temperance movement called for making the use of alcoholic beverages illegal; the movement was largely spearheaded by Frances Willard, who founded the Women's Christian Temperance Union. The suffrage movement sought to gain for women the right to vote; Elizabeth Cady Stanton (see Chapter 8) and Susan B. Anthony were leaders in that struggle.

was fond of saying that the world had two kinds of people: those who said, "Somebody ought to do something about it, but why should I?" and those who said, "Somebody must do something about it, then why not I?" Her opinion of the two groups was clear, and Alice and her siblings grew up believing that they could and should make some contribution to bettering the world in which they lived. They also grew up sharing their mother's belief in the value of personal freedom, and it is probably due in part to this early influence that all four of the Hamilton girls chose careers over marriage and family life.*

Montgomery Hamilton, Alice's father, was also a staunch supporter of his daughters' high goals for themselves. He himself had taken a classics degree from Princeton, only to yield to his father's demands that he manage the family's grocery business. Determined that his daughters should have only the best education, he kept them at home where they read history and literature for themselves, learned French and German from reading and conversation, and studied Latin and arithmetic with him or with a tutor. Since they were not confined to textbooks, they tended to choose topics of personal interest for long and intense study. That habit was to prove valuable to Alice in later years.

But all was not work at the Hamilton house. Eleven cousins joined Alice and her sisters in football games and tree climbing, and Mrs. Hamilton required long walks as a part of each day's "schooling." Alice's sisters and cousins

---

* Edith Hamilton became a renowned classics scholar, Margaret a teacher, and Nora an artist.

were her best friends and only companions, and she grew up in a sheltered world of Hamilton ideas and ideals. Those ideas met with little challenge when, at age 17, she followed her sister Edith to Mrs. Porter's School in Farmington, Connecticut. There were no required subjects at Mrs. Porter's, and Alice continued to study what she most enjoyed, avoiding the science and math she had always disliked.

Faced with choosing a career, she settled upon medicine, later explaining, "I wanted to do something that would not interfere with my freedom. I knew nothing about science but I realized that if I were a doctor, I could go anywhere I wanted—to foreign lands, to city slums—and while carrying on my profession still be of some use." Because she knew "nothing about science," she had to take remedial courses in physics and chemistry and spend part of a year in a small midwestern medical school before entering the University of Michigan, one of the few medical schools in 1892 that admitted women as well as men. There she became fascinated with a new method of diagnosing illness— a method that combined laboratory findings with a history of the patient's symptoms and experiences—and she neglected her other courses to spend extra hours in the lab.

By the time she graduated in 1893 she knew that her real interest lay in laboratory work, rather than in the conventional practice of medicine, yet she took an internship at New England Hospital for Women in Boston, and her experiences there helped to move her toward her eventual career. In Boston she worked in a slum area in which there were 13 different nationalities, and she saw, firsthand, some of the conditions Frances Willard had described to the Hamilton family over a decade earlier. She left Boston knowing that she wanted to help those people, but more than ever convinced that laboratory research was her real work.

After graduate work in Germany and at Johns Hopkins University in Baltimore, she accepted an offer to become an assistant professor of pathology at Northwestern University Medical School for Women, a position she held for five years. The offer was especially attractive because the university was in Chicago, and it was there that Alice Hamilton wanted to live—in Hull House, a settlement house established for the poor of the city some years before by Jane Addams (see Chapter 1). By fall of 1897 Hamilton was a resident of Hull House, where she made herself at home among a "family" not unlike her own, a family of strong women and sensitive, supportive men. She was to spend the next two decades of her life with Jane Addams at Hull House, and she wrote of those years:

> To me, the life there satisfied every longing for companionship, for the excitement of new experiences, for constant intellectual stimulation, and for the sense of being caught up in a big movement which enlisted my enthusiastic loyalty.

A resident at Hull House received no salary; most of those who lived there earned their living in other ways and dedicated their free time to work among their neighbors. Working out of Hull House when she was not teaching at the university, Hamilton set up a well-baby clinic that emphasized preventive health care, fought the sale and use of cocaine in the area, and taught English to immigrants applying for citizenship. She soon realized that her neighbors would remain in poverty as long as they continued to have more babies than they could care for, continued to send their children to work in the mills and factories instead of to school, and continued to be exploited by bosses who refused to pay fair wages or to provide humane working conditions.

She quickly learned that people like her Hull House neighbors did the "heavy, hot, dirty, and dangerous work of the country." At that time, workers in Chicago's steel mills worked 7 days a week, 12 hours a day for pitiful wages. They were expected to work until they dropped of exhaustion, had an accident, or caused trouble. Then they were fired and others were hired in their places. There seemed to be an endless supply of immigrant workers, and no one protested the low wages, since they seemed high compared to what the laborers had earned in their old countries.

Troubled by stories of illnesses that she suspected stemmed from the work these men and women were doing, Hamilton read Sir Thomas Oliver's *Dangerous Trades* and discovered that the dangers of the workplace were common knowledge in England and that most European countries had already done much to improve conditions for their working people. But she could find no articles on the topic in American journals. Most people seemed to believe that American factories were far superior to those in Europe and there was therefore little cause for concern.

Hamilton's work among the people of Hull House convinced her that this was not the case, and she began to investigate the problem on her own. In 1906 she wrote an article noting that tuberculosis was more common among workers at certain jobs, notably those she called "the dusty trades." Two years later, she published a description of several job-related illnesses and noted that the diseases of which she wrote were most often found among "a class which . . . is compelled to a great extent to follow certain trades, and to work in certain places, and has very little choice." Clearly somebody needed to do something about the problems of these people, and Alice Hamilton knew well the phrase "Then why not I?"

She seized the first opportunity. In 1907 the state of Illinois had formed a commission to identify and study the dangerous trades, and by 1910 Alice Hamilton was director of that commission. At the age of 40 she began the work for which she had, unknowingly, spent a lifetime in preparation, a work that enabled her to bring laboratory science directly into the lives of working men and women. She entered a field that had, as yet, no followers in the United States—the field of industrial medicine. Within that field she turned her energies to industrial toxicology, the study of the ill effects that toxic, or poisonous, substances in the workplace have upon factory workers.

She set out to study lead, since plumbism, or lead poisoning, was a major threat to the health of workers in several large industries in Illinois. But where should she begin? Most hospital records of victims of plumbism held no clue as to the patient's occupation, and the records of doctors and nurses working in the factories sometimes actually covered up the facts she was seeking.

Alice Hamilton turned to the people. She talked to the workers themselves on visits to paint-making plants, lead smelters and refineries, storage-battery factories, and enameling works. She went into saloons in the roughest sections of cities in order to interview workers who suffered from lead poisoning. She went to priests, visiting nurses, druggists, and others who might know of cases of plumbism, and she went to the wives of working men. The women proved a most valuable source, one of them confiding,

> We all knew you was coming. They've been cleaning up for you something fierce. Why in the room where my husband works they tore out the ceiling, because they couldn't cover up the red lead. And a doctor came and looked at all the men and them that's got lead, forty of them, has got to keep to home the day you're there.

Hamilton's doggedness was rewarded, and she recorded hundreds of cases of plumbism.*

Even in the face of such findings, Dr. Hamilton had no authority to force employers to make needed improvements, for her official duties were limited to the filing of written reports. Fully aware that reports could be too easily filed and forgotten, she took her facts directly to the bosses, making sure they understood full well the suffering of the workers exposed to lead in their plants and trying to convince them that keeping workers healthy and on the job was to their advantage.

---

* One case, typical of numerous others, involved a Bohemian who worked as an enameler of bathtubs, pouring lead powder over red-hot tubs as they came from a furnace. After a year and a half on the job, he fainted and lapsed into a four-day coma. Weeks of delirium and palsy followed.

Most factory owners seemed ignorant of the harm their plants were causing and were ready enough to make needed changes. There were even those cases in which factory owners did far more than Hamilton originally recommended, striving to make their plants models for the industry. But there were other owners who seemed to care far more for the money they were making than for the human beings who worked in their factories.

Alice Hamilton knew that only laws could force some employers to do what others were willing to do voluntarily, and she worked for the passage of Illinois's Occupational Disease Act of 1911, one of the first of its kind in the nation. That act improved working conditions for some, but there were loopholes in it that allowed many businesses to continue their dangerous practices. And Illinois was one of only six states that had such a law. In other parts of the country, conditions in the workplace were as bad as ever, and when Alice Hamilton traveled to Brussels to deliver a paper at the International Congress on Industrial Hygiene, she found out just how far behind the United States was in the field.

While her Illinois survey showed that one out of every seven men working with white lead, a particularly toxic form of the metal, showed signs of lead poisoning, a report from England showed that only one worker out of 264 in that country suffered from the disease. In one American plant that employed 85 men she had found 35 "leaded," while an English plant employing 90 men had not had a single case of lead poisoning in the past five years. Furthermore, some of the cases of plumbism she described were so severe that European doctors told her they had only read about such cases—in files from the nineteenth century.

Clearly something had to be done. And Alice Hamilton was, again, the one to do it. Charles Neill, U.S. Commissioner of Labor, was at the Brussels meeting and heard Alice Hamilton speak. He approached her with an offer to conduct a special government investigation into the dangerous trades, starting with lead, and she immediately accepted that challenge. What had started as a single woman's effort to change the lives of workers was building into a national force.

But the force lacked real strength, for there were no federal laws compelling employers to provide safe working conditions for their employees. Again Hamilton relied on her persuasive abilities to bring about needed changes. A relatively shy woman who hated conflict, she often had to push herself past a simple explanation of the facts to force a commitment for change from an employer.

An employer's responsibility for the health of his workers was a new concept in 1911; a typical response to an Alice Hamilton report came from an owner who asked her, "Do you mean to say that if a man gets poisoned in my place I am to be held responsible?" Others pushed for proof of their responsibility, and Hamilton set out to establish beyond question the cause-and-effect relationship between work on a job site and subsequent illness or death.

In order to do so, she had to study every aspect of a manufacturing or refining process so that she knew every chemical used or created as a waste product. And she had to see those operations firsthand—no matter how dangerous her investigation might prove to be. As one journalist noted, she was remembered by many laborers as "a slender, tweed-clad figure walking . . . on narrow planks hundreds of feet above the ground alongside of vats of seething sulphuric acid; dropping down vertical ladders into the dense darkness of copper mines. . . ."

Though she had begun with lead industries, she soon extended her investigation to other areas; she found that such jobs as glazing and decorating tiles and pottery, enameling bathtubs and sinks, making coffin trim, polishing cut glass, compounding rubber, and typesetting all carried the danger of plumbism. She learned over the years that in these, as in other industries, health hazards often came from more than one source. Enamel workers who poured lead dust over bathtubs and sinks usually worked for no more than three to four years before dying—either from lead poisoning or from tuberculosis or other lung diseases related to the ingestion of silica dust. Stone cutters who used pneumatic drills suffered from "dead fingers," caused by the drill's vibration, as well as from lung diseases stemming from the dust they breathed. Workers in the rubber industry were in danger of lead poisoning, of cyanosis caused by breathing solvents, and of a form of insanity known as carbon disulphide psychosis.

Alice Hamilton faced a moral dilemma when the United States government asked her to head a study of the hazards associated with the production of weapons during World War I. For several years Hamilton had been active in the women's peace movement in which her friend Jane Addams was a leading force. In spring of 1915 she had joined Addams as a delegate to a meeting in The Hague; there, with 1,135 other women from 12 different countries she pledged herself to the cause of peace. How could an avowed pacifist devote her energies to the inspection of factories dedicated to the production of weapons? Years later she justified her role in investigating the war industries as having accomplished a "good deal" more than her anti-war protests.

Conditions in the war industries were unusually dangerous, for the production of TNT and other munitions materials was new to this country, and workers had become human guinea pigs. Hamilton's work was made doubly difficult by the war-time secrecy attached to the plants she investigated. Often even their locations were not public knowledge, and since the government was not particularly interested in aiding an investigation that might hamper the war effort, even the Commissioner of Labor himself could not direct Hamilton to the plants. She had to find them on her own. The picric acid and nitrocellulose plants where explosives were being made were easy to locate—she had only to follow the yellow-orange plumes of nitrous fumes, which killed the vegetation for miles around and could cause instant death if inhaled directly. But locating the plants was only half the battle. "The industrial world seemed to be given over to a sort of joyous ruthlessness," Hamilton later recalled, and only her great powers of persuasion began to change the hazardous conditions and save the lives of the workers.

By 1919 her work had come to the attention of the staff of Harvard Medical School, and she was invited to do a lecture series that spring. To her surprise, she was then offered a fall appointment teaching industrial medicine, noting later, "I was really about the only candidate available." She would be the first woman faculty member and as such could not expect to use the Harvard Club, demand her quota of football tickets, or march in the commencement procession. Against these conditions, Hamilton set several of her own: she was to be allowed to return for one half of every year to Hull House, continue her work for the Bureau of Labor, and have a free hand in selecting the areas in which she conducted her research. The terms were agreed upon by both sides, and she began her work at Harvard. Despite her considerable achievement there, she never rose above the rank of assistant professor. At her retirement in 1935, she was awarded the rank of professor emeritus, which she declared "a great honor [that] pleasantly ignores my sex."

That same year, Hamilton took up a new life in Hadlyme Ferry, Connecticut, in a house she had bought for herself and her sisters. Retirement from Harvard had simply freed her to engage in more consulting work in the dangerous trades and to lecture more widely on the importance of protecting the health of the worker. Her sister Margaret, a retired teacher, moved in with her, and the two entertained guests who shared their interests in improving the quality of human life.

There were some whose interests Alice Hamilton did not endorse. She opposed an equal rights amendment proposed first in the 1920s and again in the 1940s. Her opposition had nothing to do with lack of sympathy for the feminist cause. She had been a leader in the birth control movement, was an enthusiastic supporter of suffrage, and had fought to eliminate working conditions that were especially hazardous to women. In fact, it was because she had seen,

Alice Hamilton as a medical student

Alice Hamilton of the Harvard College faculty

firsthand, the powerlessness of American women to protect themselves in the marketplace that she opposed the equal rights amendment. She feared employers would use such an amendment to erase all the benefits that had been so hard won. She held that stance until 1952 when improved labor conditions in America finally led her to give her support to the amendment.

Alice Hamilton's contributions to her profession brought her many honors in her later years, including the Lasker Award from the American Health Association for "combating the most frequent causes of death and disease." When asked about such honors, she invariably remarked that she felt her greatest tribute came from a smelting expert who noted that "here is a woman writing on the metallurgy of lead who knows her job perfectly."

Alice Hamilton had learned as a child the art of doing a job perfectly, of finding out everything there was to know about a subject. And she had given most of her life to putting those skills to work in a new field. As a colleague said upon the occasion of her ninetieth birthday, "Industrial medicine today is Alice Hamilton's early dream come true." But Hamilton herself was never satisfied that her goals had been accomplished. Though she lived long enough to see the enactment of worker's compensation laws across the nation, she died a few months before President Richard Nixon signed the Occupational Safety and Health Act of 1970, an act that at last gave the federal government the power to intervene when employers failed to provide safe working conditions for their employees. But even that act would not have satisfied Alice Hamilton completely, for she foresaw that the rapid increase in the use of newly compounded chemicals would continue to cast the worker in the role of "guinea pig."

Nonetheless, her efforts to combat such practices had changed the character of American industry. When she died of a stroke on September 22, 1970, those who knew of her great contributions could remember with satisfaction the tribute President Nixon had paid her a year and a half earlier on her one hundredth birthday: "I know of no one who can look with greater satisfaction on so many decades of selfless, ungrudging service to humanity."

5

She Dared to Help Break the Chains

"*M*<i>a, they're coming!" Without turning her gaze from
the horizon, the five-year-old almost whispered the
words to the woman who was stooped beside her, loosen-
ing the soil and then worrying it up into small mounds.
Quickly the woman straightened, shaded her eyes, and
looked in the direction the little girl indicated. "You're
right, Mary," she said. "Now take your little brothers inside and keep them as quiet as you can. It'll be all right
now. You'll see."

Flinging one last look down the road by which the small
cadre of brightly uniformed soldiers was approaching,
Mary quickly pulled the two small boys from their play.
Taking one by each hand and shushing their protests, she
herded them toward the one-room straw-and-sod cottage.
Pushing them through the door, she settled them in a far
corner and set a small tin of smooth stones in front of them,
hoping against hope that the collection of pebbles would
hold their interest for at least a little while.

Tiptoeing back to the doorway, Mary peered out to see her mother still busily engaged with the potato planting, pretending to be unaware of the British soldiers marching toward her. Mary would not cry. She had promised her father that she would be a big girl and help her mother until they could all be together again. But what if the soldiers hurt her mother, like they'd promised to hurt her father?

As she watched, the men drew to a halt in front of the cottage and their leader hailed her mother. Rising slowly, Mrs. Harris straightened her skirts and faced them, but made no other move.

"We're here to arrest Richard Harris by order of His Majesty the King," the soldier shouted from the roadway.

"My husband's not here," Mary heard her mother say.

The leader turned to the others. "Search the place," he said, and with that the men broke rank and moved toward the cottage. At the same time Mrs. Harris dropped her trowel, lifted up her skirts, and hurried toward the house, reaching Mary just ahead of the soldiers. Making no attempt to block the doorway, she simply nudged Mary across the threshold and toward the corner where the small boys sat, their attention riveted now on the commotion at the door.

As Mary watched from her mother's side, the soldiers swept clumsily through the room, pulling the curtain from the window, upsetting the crude table, and sending bowls and cups clattering to the floor.

"The chimney," the officer said, gesturing toward the small hearth.

The soldier standing nearest the fireplace knelt down and peered up the chimney. "I can't see anything," he said.

"*Tear it down,*" *his commander ordered. Mrs. Harris gasped and Mary pressed more closely to her side, as two of the soldiers raised their rifle butts and began to pound at the crudely mortared stones. Helpless, Mary watched in horror as the soldiers destroyed the wall.*

"*I told you he wasn't here.*" *The firmness of her mother's voice somehow reassured Mary. "You'll never find him if you search all of Ireland.*"

A soldier raised his hand as if to strike the woman, but the officer waved him off. Stepping over the rubble, he ushered his men out of the cottage and ordered them into formation on the road outside.

Inside mother and children stood motionless amid the ruins. "You were strong, Mary," said Mrs. Harris as she knelt to gather the two little boys into her arms. "That is good. They'll not likely be botherin' us again."

Mary made no answer. Her eyes were fixed on the wall where the chimney had once stood, for through the gaping hole she could still see the disappearing backs of the British soldiers.

The scene seared itself into the memory of the little girl. Three quarters of a century later and an ocean away, Mary Harris, now "Mother Jones," the fiery leader of America's discontented workers would proclaim, "I was born in revolution. . . . I belong to a class which has been robbed, exploited, and plundered down through many long centuries. And . . . I have an impulse to . . . help break the chains."

Mary Harris was born on May 1, 1830,* in County Cork, Ireland, the first child of Richard and Helen Harris. Her father, like his father before him, was deeply involved in the movement for Irish independence. But unlike her grandfather, who was caught and hanged, Mary's father escaped the British tyranny and in 1835 slipped out of Ireland, making his way to America and vowing that as soon as he had enough money to do so, he would send for his family.

Left behind in troubled Ireland with three little children to care for, Mary's mother worked their small acreage, using her hands and her wits to provide for the family. In America, Richard Harris found work building the railroads and canals that were opening up the young nation to new settlement and new industry. He worked hard, and in six years he had earned his American citizenship and had saved enough money to send for his family.

Mary Harris was 11 years old when she, her mother, and two younger brothers packed their meager belongings, traveled the short distance to the city of Cork, and boarded the immigrant ship that brought them to America. Along with other Irish families making the ocean voyage, they spent the next four weeks huddled in the hold of the vessel, with no room to stretch, no fresh air to breathe, impure water to drink, insufficient food to eat, and little to sustain them save their dreams of a better life in their new country.

---

* The year of her birth is not certain, but 1830 is the date most generally accepted.

By the time his family arrived in America, Richard Harris's work on the railroad had taken him to Toronto, Ontario, and it was there that Mary, an American citizen by virtue of her father's citizenship, spent the rest of her youth, "without luxuries," she later said, "but also without wants." Shortly after the family settled in Toronto, the city opened its first free public schools, and the young Harrises were enrolled by their parents, who were determined to give them the education they themselves had never had the chance to obtain. An excellent student, Mary advanced quickly through the grades, graduating from high school in 1847. Unable to attend Toronto's new teacher-training school because she was a woman, she became a dressmaker, working out of the family home.

When the teacher-training school did open its doors to women three years later, Mary enrolled, but as a Roman Catholic she was barred from teaching in Toronto. At age 22, Mary Harris left home, determined to find a place in the world where she could live and work as she wished. She spent time in Maine as a private tutor, then taught for a year in a convent school in Michigan before moving on to the promise of young, vibrant Chicago, Queen City of the Midwest. There she was able to support herself comfortably as a seamstress. But she still considered teaching her natural vocation, and when Memphis, Tennessee, advertised for teachers, 30-year-old Mary Harris left Chicago and made her way south.

It was the summer of 1860 and Memphis, a river town and a rail center, was booming. Mary easily found a teaching job and took a room in a ghetto area off Catfish Bay, a neighborhood known to the citizens of Memphis as Pinch-gut, or Pinch, because of the emaciated look of the Irish immigrants living there. Soon after she settled into her new life, Mary Harris met George Jones, an ironworker in a Memphis foundry, and they were married late that fall, a scant two months after their first meeting.

The next few years were happy ones for the Joneses. Living in one of Pinch's big, old houses, they were relatively unaffected by the turmoil of the Civil War that engulfed the country and the city. Northern sympathizers, they rejoiced when Memphis fell to the Union army within a year of the outbreak of the war.

Emancipation gave promise of new life to blacks. At the same time, unionism, a movement of laborers who joined together to secure better wages and working conditions, was bringing promise of new life to the families of Pinch. When workers in Memphis heard that an ironworker's union, the first of its kind, had been formed in Philadelphia, George Jones helped organize a Memphis branch of the Iron Molders Union. Caught up in the dream of a better life, he eventually became a full-time union organizer, traveling throughout the South to encourage other iron-workers to establish their own local unions, promising the men a brighter future if they worked together to help themselves and each other.

Seven years married, with four happy, healthy children, Mary and George Jones felt their own future was full of promise. Then in the fall of 1867, following an exception-ally wet spring and a hot, humid summer, yellow fever, carried by the mosquitoes that abounded under such conditions, struck the city of Memphis. Within a week Mary Harris Jones had lost her husband and all her children to the dread, uncontrollable disease. Later she described the tragedy:

> One by one, my four little children sickened and died. I sat alone through nights of grief. No one came to me. No one could. Other houses were as stricken as mine. All day long, all night long, I heard the grating of the wheels of the death cart.

But Mary Jones was not one to sit helplessly, hopelessly by. Seeing the great suffering and need around her, she promptly applied for a permit to enter quarantined homes and help the other families who were afflicted with the disease that had destroyed her own. She bathed feverish and delirious victims, fed those who could eat, and took care of children whose parents lay dying.

By December of 1867 the plague had burned itself out, and Mary Harris, 37 years old and a childless widow, packed her few possessions and left Memphis, heading north to Chicago where she set up a storefront dressmaking shop on the city's west end. But fate had one more blow for Mary Jones. In October of 1871 the great bustling city of Chicago was all but destroyed by a catastrophic fire that raged unchecked for three days, leaving more than 300 people dead and 90,000 homeless. Having lost her shop and all her possessions in the fire, Mary Jones was among the army of homeless. Moving into the basement of a church that served as a temporary shelter for refugees of the fire, she quickly busied herself helping other victims of the tragedy. As had been the case in Memphis, she healed her own wounds by binding those of others.

She was 41 years old the year of the fire, and she would live almost another 60 years, but Mary Harris Jones would never again attempt to establish a home of her own. For the rest of her life, she would stay wherever she found shelter, explaining in later years, "I live in the United States. But I do not know exactly where. . . . My address is like my shoes: it travels with me." Living without property and without bank accounts, she would sometimes have income from union activities, but more often she would simply depend upon friends to supply whatever necessities she lacked. Over the years she would make her home in steel-workers' shanties and in the flimsy dwellings of a tent city thrown up by coal miners on strike. For sometime during the months following the Chicago fire, Mary Jones wandered into a meeting of the Knights of Labor and realized that all the hope left to her and to others of the working class lay within that smoke-blackened hall.

The events of the last few years had made her acutely aware of the indifference of the wealthy class to the sufferings of the poor. In Memphis, deaths from yellow fever had been largely confined to poor neighborhoods. The rich had been able to leave the city and escape the plague. In Chicago, she had observed the vast difference in lifestyle between the two classes of people with whom she was most familiar—the wealthy people whose fine clothes she sewed and the struggling immigrant families who were her neighbors. There were two camps, she said, "the working people on one side—hungry, cold, jobless—and the employers on the other, knowing neither hunger nor cold."

Everything around her made Mary Jones aware that America's working people—those who dug the nation's coal, forged its steel, and worked in its factories—did not share the nation's growing wealth. All too often, they led wretched lives in deplorable housing, working for starvation wages under nightmarish conditions.

Seized by a growing conviction that something had to be done to set the American system to rights, Mary Jones joined forces with the Knights of Labor, becoming a "supporter," since women at that time could not be members, and listing her trade as "dressmaker." Fascinated by what she saw and heard at the Knights of Labor meetings, she began to spend more and more time at the hall, "listening to splendid speakers." A silent observer at first, she soon grew more familiar with the Knights and their program and began to speak out, urging the members to bring more workers into the movement, urging them to ever greater commitment to the cause. Known around the union hall as the lady "with the quick brain and even quicker tongue," Mary Jones was soon being asked to go to different parts of the city and speak to groups of working men.

She gained quick fame, simply because she was such an unusual figure in the labor movement. She was not only a woman, but she was a most unlikely looking woman to be addressing groups of rough workingmen. She was small, but sturdy—less than five feet in height, but a solid 100 pounds in weight. Always conscious of her appearance, she wore sedate black dresses trimmed with a touch of lace or color. A jaunty black bonnet was perched on top of her snow-white hair, and blue eyes shone from her handsome

Irish face. A well-educated woman and a particularly well-spoken one, she often shocked more genteel audiences with her command of a workingman's language. She had a low and pleasant voice, and there was an intensity in her speech and a fluidity to her phrases that made audiences listen and believe.

Her message was simple: an individual worker was powerless, but even the most unscrupulous employer could not ignore collective strength. In Chicago, in Pittsburgh, in textile towns, and in isolated mining camps, Mary Jones delivered that message to the workingmen and their families who struggled against the harsh conditions of life. Tracing her activities through the next two decades is difficult. Her own writings do not attach dates to her wanderings, and her name was not yet sufficiently recognizable to call her to the attention of the reporters who were covering the increasing unrest among the nation's struggling workers. But by the early 1890s stories of the cruel and bloody strikes that were breaking out in the coal fields of West Virginia and Pennsylvania spoke of the "courageous" or "villainous" acts of a diminutive woman called "Mother Jones" by the miners. In that desolate hill country where miners and their families eked out an existence, she was leading the fight against the cruel conditions the large coal companies imposed on their workers. She was "Mother Jones" and the coal miners were "her boys." This special relationship would last the rest of her life. For though she worked for all aspects of the cause of labor, her greatest compassion seemed to be evoked by the coal miners.

Certainly the miners had need of her. Mining was, in Mother Jones's own words, "cruel work . . . hard and ugly." Miners worked 12 to 14 hours a day, six days a week in dark, poorly ventilated pits deep in the earth. Stooped and bent, they picked and shoveled coal and loaded it by hand onto carts pulled in and out of the mine by donkeys or dogs. Cave-ins were a constant threat, and explosions were common. Mother Jones saw the newly organized United Mine Workers of America as the miners' only hope of changing such conditions. Moving through the coal fields of northern and southern West Virginia and into the anthracite mines of Pennsylvania, she carried the gospel of the United Mine Workers.

Her words brought new hope to immigrants and displaced farmers who had been lured to the mines with the promise of free land. When the promised land failed to materialize, the coal miners and their families, too poor to move on, settled into bleak and hopeless lives in "company towns" near the mines. Those grim settlements were generally composed of rows of shanties, a school, a church, and a store, all owned and controlled by the company and all located on company land. Often as not, the miners were paid in scrip, the company's own paper money, rather than in federal currency, so there was no saving ahead for escape, even if wages had been high enough to allow for saving. And a miner paid a high price for voicing his discontent. "Men who joined the union were blacklisted," Mother Jones noted in her autobiography. "Their families thrown out [of their homes]. Men were shot . . . beaten. Many disappeared without a trace. Storekeepers were ordered not to sell to union men or their families."

It was this life that Mother Jones shared with the miners. She lived with miners' families in the shanties of company towns. She organized meetings at crossroads when companies would not allow miners to gather on company land. She drank with the miners in taverns. She talked their language. She stamped her feet; she shouted, gestured, scolded, and shamed them, urging them to join the union, to seek change through collective strength. She shook workers out of their apathy and fear. She gave them energy; she gave them conviction. As one reporter observed, "With one speech she [could throw] a whole community on strike and she could keep the strikers loyal month after month on empty stomachs and behind prison bars."

She earned that loyalty by suffering the empty stomach and standing behind the prison bars with them, declaring, "to be in prison is no disgrace." She went, in her own words, "wherever there was a good fight against wrong," despite the fact that "outside organizers" who went into mining districts were often brutally beaten by company guards and hired thugs. Protected by her sex and her courage, the little woman in black moved fearlessly among the camps, at one time walking up to a guard and placing her hand over the barrel of the machine gun he had aimed at her.

She devised ingenious tactics by which to bring strikes to successful conclusions. When "scabs," or strikebreakers, once kept the Pennsylvania mines operating through five long months of strike, the miners despaired of ever forcing the owners to consider their demands. But Mother Jones arrived, assessed the situation, and took action. Organizing the miners' wives into a ragtag army bearing brooms, mops, and tin washtubs, she marched them to the mine entrance. The terrible din of the washtub band and the unusual appearance of the women so frightened the mules and so unnerved the scabs that all mining activities ceased. The women maintained this unusual picket line at the mine entrance until the company capitulated and agreed to meet with the miners to discuss their grievances.

The miners won that strike for shorter hours, better pay, and the right to unionize, but Mother Jones and her followers lost more often than they won in those early days. Still, defeat in a strike never seemed to dishearten the intrepid little woman. She never lost faith in the rightness of the cause or in the ultimate victory of the worker. She often compared the workers' plight to that of the slaves and spoke of the labor movement as a latter-day Civil War. She knew that though striking workers might lose a particular battle and be forced to accept a less than satisfactory settlement, the war would continue until justice was won.

Though she came to be known as "the miners' angel," her concern was by no means limited to coal miners. Once, while visiting a coal field near Birmingham, Alabama, Mother Jones came across a textile factory staffed almost entirely by children. Boys and girls as young as six worked an eight-hour day for a dime, untangling thread on whirling spindles and crawling through machinery to oil and clean the works. Accidents were frequent and tragic. Shocked by these conditions, Mother Jones went through the South, taking jobs in factories in Georgia, South Carolina, and Alabama, observing the tragedy of labor forced on children.

But conditions of child labor were no better in the North.

When the textile workers of the Kensington mills outside Philadelphia went out on strike in 1903, Mother Jones noted that of the 100,000 strikers, 16,000 were young children. Though Pennsylvania had a child labor law that prohibited children under the age of 13 from working, the companies held such great political power that the law was never enforced. But Mother Jones had no fear of the wealth and power of mill owners. Determined to bring the situation to the attention of the entire nation, she organized the March of the Mill Children in the summer of 1903. With 300 marchers, 200 of them children between the ages of 8 and 11, she set off from Kensington, Pennsylvania, bound for Sagamore Hill, the summer estate of President Theodore Roosevelt at Oyster Bay, Long Island. As she later explained, she felt it would be beneficial for the president to "see these mill children and compare them with his own little ones who were spending the summer at the seashore." The 125-mile, 22-day march was covered in its entirety by the *New York Times*. The front-page story drew Mother Jones all the national attention she could have wished for, and still Teddy Roosevelt did not open the gates of his estate to Mother Jones and her little band of children, nor would he carry her fight to Congress.*

Defeated but undaunted, Mother Jones continued her fight against economic injustice. She spent the first two decades of the twentieth century crisscrossing the continent, participating in strikes, fund-raisers, and confer-

---

* The first federal child labor law was not passed until 1941, 11 years after the death of Mother Jones and nearly 40 years after the March of the Mill Children.

ences, always speaking out for the workers' cause. She joined with union efforts in the copper mines of Michigan, Arizona, and Montana. She was involved in strikes of garment workers in Chicago, New York, and Philadelphia, of brewery workers in Milwaukee, of steelworkers in Pittsburgh, of factory workers in New Jersey, and of railroad workers on the west coast. She joined strikes in Canada and worked to organize the miners of Mexico. She testified before special congressional committees. She had private interviews with John D. Rockefeller, Jr., with governors, and with presidents.

Wherever the fight was the fiercest, Mother Jones was there to aid, organize, and encourage. Day and night, in poor villages, in tent cities, in lonely cabins, and in crowded ghettos, Mother Jones brought solace, defied police lines, used disguises to slip in and out of guarded strike zones, raised funds, and did all she could to make the nation aware of the lonely struggle of the working class. A key issue in that struggle was the right of the workers to organize and bargain collectively, and she considered a failure any strike that did not gain the employer's recognition of that right.*

Believing that violence only produced violence and that what was "won today by violence will be lost tomorrow," she nonetheless urged miners to arm themselves, because "no one should be helpless in the face of brute force." While she denied claims that she preached peace and raised

---

* Mother Jones died before a 1931 federal law finally guaranteed Americans the right to form unions.

Mother Jones leading the March of the Mill Children

Mother Jones at 75

war, she admitted she was no pacifist.* Introduced once as "a great humanitarian," she promptly rose and said, "Get it right. I'm not a humanitarian. I'm a hell-raiser." But in all her crusades she was only invoking the laws of the land —the American freedoms of speech and of assembly.

Rather than diminishing her zeal, the passing years seemed to add fuel to her fervor. She remained active until almost the very end of her 100 years of life. At 93 she began *The Autobiography of Mother Jones*, a book that tells her story almost as colorfully as she lived it. At 94 she made her last address to a union convention. At 100, she celebrated her birthday in the farm home of a retired miner and his wife in Silver Spring, Maryland, and an "army" of workers who were camped at the White House to protest the plight of the poor marched eight miles to the farm to pay her tribute. John D. Rockefeller, Jr., her adversary in bitter and bloody strikes in the Colorado mines, sent her a congratulatory telegram: "Your loyalty to your ideas, your fearless adherence to your duty as you have seen it is an inspiration to all who have known you."

Six months later, on November 30, 1930, she was dead. At a requiem mass at St. Gabriel's in Washington, D.C., eight men representing eight different organized trades served as her pallbearers. A special railway car carried the

---

* Mother Jones was a one-issue woman. She gave no support to social reform movements such as pacifism, temperance, and suffrage. Though she had wielded tremendous influence in many political campaigns, she did not consider the vote an essential right for women, maintaining, "I have never had a vote and I have raised hell all over this country. You don't need a vote to raise hell. You need conviction and a voice."

simple casket to Mount Olive, a little town in the coal fields of southern Illinois. After lying in state for three days, her body was taken to a miner's graveyard and lowered into the earth next to some of "her boys." "She was a sweet old lady . . . a scrapper. You couldn't have helped loving her," said a bystander.

Mother Jones, the lady who had once been called "the most dangerous woman in America," was gone. No monuments were erected to her, and yet she changed the lives of millions of American workers. For when they had no hope, she inspired them, and when they thought no one cared, she was there. Her monuments were, in effect, the hope, the courage, and the dreams she gave to the American worker. "Slowly," she closed her autobiography, "those who create the wealth of the world are permitted to share it. The future is in labor's strong, rough hands."

6

She Dared to
Play Out the Stories

"*W*hen the chief saw Eleanor rush into her mother's arms, he said, 'Go, Little Sister. It is time for you to return to your people. I will keep you from them no more.' And so after four years with the Seneca tribe, your Great-Grandmother Eleanor Lytle Kinzie returned to her parents and learned once more the ways of the white child.*"

"*What did you say her Indian name was?*" asked Daisy.

"*Little-Ship-Under-Full-Sail,*" answered Grandmother Kinzie. "*Because she was such a little girl to be so full of energy.*"

"*Why didn't she run away home?*" asked Daisy. "*I'm nine, just the same as she was when they captured her, and I wouldn't have let any Indians keep me away from my Papa and Mama.*"

"*But the chief made her his sister,*" said 11-year-old Eleanor, feeling more than two years wiser than her sister.

"*I guess that would have been all right, but I still would have wanted to go home to Papa,*" *Daisy said.*

"*You should be going up to tell your Papa good-night right now,*" *said Grandmother Kinzie.* "*It's past your bedtime.*"

"*Not yet!*" *said Daisy, unwilling to have the storytelling over so soon.* "*First tell us the story about wearing the knife and tin cup on your belt. Tell us the one about the blizzard.*"

"*Yes, yes!*" *begged four-year-old Alice.*

"*Well, all right,*" *Grandmother Kinzie agreed.* "*But first let me poke up the fire. This is a cold, cold story.*"

Daisy handed her the poker, then settled down to wait for the magic words that would take them back to the days when their grandmother was first married, the days when Indians rode freely across the Great Plains and white settlers carved out new lives in the wilderness.

And though the hour was late and her eyes grew heavy, Daisy missed not a word of the story, for she knew that tomorrow she and her sisters would go out to the farthest edge of the Kinzie woods and play out the stories, reliving the old adventures in the wonderful world of make-believe where grown-ups almost never go.

It was a game young Daisy never tired of, and it was a world she kept open for many girls and reopened for their grown-up leaders. For Daisy was the nickname of Juliette Gordon Low, founder of the Girl Scouts of America, and fortunately for the thousands of girls who took up Scouting, she was one of those rare adults who never gave up her childhood games.

Christened Juliette Kinzie after the courageous Chicago grandmother whose stories of Indians and blizzards so delighted her, Juliette Gordon was called Daisy almost from her birth on October 31, 1860. Her father, William Washington Gordon II, gave her the name, and her older sister often called her "Crazy Daisy," because she was so unpredictable.

Daisy grew up in an unpredictable world. Her earliest memories of childhood in Savannah, Georgia, were of a world of uniformed soldiers, for her father was an officer in the Confederate army and the women of the Gordon family spent many an hour discussing war news. For Daisy's mother, Eleanor Kinzie Gordon, the war years were doubly difficult because her own parents were Yankees, and her brothers fought for the North. For years the six Gordon children, Eleanor, Daisy, Alice, Bill, Mabel, and Arthur, played out the Civil War in games and dramas with their many cousins. Always Daisy was a leading figure in their playacting, for she had a keen enjoyment of the world of "let's pretend." During summers at Etowah Cliffs in northern Georgia, Daisy directed her many cousins as they turned a rocky outcropping into the Castle of Redcliffe and played at being lords and ladies or wandered through the pine forests reliving scenes from Grandmother Kinzie's stories of campfires and Indian raids.

And there were imaginative worlds to be explored on paper, as well. Daisy's poems and drawings frequently appeared in the *Malbone Bouquet*, a monthly newspaper begun by her cousin Caroline. The girls were disappointed when *St. Nicholas*, the famous children's magazine, rejected

"The Months," an illustrated poem the *Malbone Bouquet* had found perfectly suitable, but they continued to write for their own publication. Daisy's writing was encouraged by Grandmother Kinzie, who had gained some fame as the author of a book containing many of the Indian stories she told to her grandchildren. When Juliette Kinzie died, ten-year-old Daisy felt a great loss, and she spent much of the rest of her life trying to recapture the adventure that seemed to go out of her life that summer of 1870.

At 13 Daisy was sent to boarding school in Virginia where she read English history and literature and steeped herself in the lore of castles and kings. Three years later, she followed her sister Eleanor to the Mesdemoiselles Charbonnier's School in New York City, a school so strict that the girls were required to speak only in French and were never allowed outside the building except in the company of their teachers. Daisy was granted an exception to that rule in order to take painting lessons from a famous artist, and her drawings and paintings earned her enough recognition to offset the problems caused by her poor efforts in spelling and math.

Despite the fact that she was a regular reader of a strange publication called *The Ugly Girl Papers* and was constantly worrying about the size of her nose, Daisy made a successful social debut in Savannah and enjoyed an impressive number of parties held in her honor. Shortly thereafter, she returned to "The Charbs" in New York to continue her study of painting and to be company to her younger sister Alice. When Alice died suddenly of complications from scarlet fever that year, the family was thrown into deep grieving.

Partly to save Daisy from her mother's preoccupation with Alice's death, Willie Gordon sent his second daughter on a round of visits to various friends and relatives. This proved to be the beginning of nearly four years of such wanderings, years that included two trips to Europe where she met William MacKay Low, the son of a Scotsman who had made a fortune in the cotton business. Remembering her father's advice to choose a poor man who had made his way up over a rich man who had never learned to appreciate his wealth, Daisy kept her attraction to Willie Low a secret until she was practically engaged. Though not totally approving the match, Mr. Gordon did not prevent it, and after a lavish wedding in Savannah, Daisy and Willie left for a honeymoon on a nearby island. Two days later they were back in Savannah, for a piece of wedding rice had lodged itself in Daisy's ear and caused an abscess that made her deaf in that ear and severely limited her hearing in the other. From that day, Crazy Daisy was to seem more eccentric than ever, for when she did not understand what was said to her, she either ignored it entirely or tried to imagine what had been said and act accordingly. Neither practice earned her a reputation for predictable behavior.

Once settled in England, Daisy Gordon Low was an instant social success. She already knew a great many people from her previous summers abroad, and her Southern sense of hospitality made her a favorite with everyone from the Prince of Wales to Rudyard Kipling. She moved easily among British dignitaries, and she enjoyed introducing them to the delights of Southern cooking, carried out by a cook she brought with her from Savannah. Back and forth she traveled, spending time in England, in Georgia, and with friends and relatives in New York and Washington, D.C. Her life was one long cycle of parties and entertainments—from hunting deer with her husband in the woods of Scotland to planning her sister's debutante cotillion in Savannah.

Her most adventuresome work was undertaken on behalf of a project instigated by her mother—a hospital for typhoid fever victims who were serving under Brigadier General William Gordon. Gordon, now 64 years old, had put aside his grudge against the United States government to accept a commission and command a post in Florida during the Spanish-American War of 1898. His wife had noted the lack of proper facilities for sick and injured soldiers and had goaded the government into supplying better care for its military men.

But aside from this brief period of intense commitment to a cause, Daisy's life was given over to playing English lady. What else had her life and education prepared her for? Her mother and her Grandmother Gordon had spent their lives as proper wives and mothers, and now she was to do the same. But she had no children. And Willy Low's interest in her began to fade with the passing of the years. Eventually he demanded a divorce so that he could marry a widow with whom he'd been traveling, and Daisy found herself caught up in events over which she had very little control. In 1905, before divorce proceedings were final, Willy died, leaving a confusing will that took several years to settle.

During that time Daisy worried constantly over money, for never having had a limit to her income, she had never learned to operate within a budget. Even as she fretted, she often gave money away to people in need, forgetting that she no longer possessed limitless resources. Her poor math confused matters further, for she never was quite sure how much money was left for necessities and travel. Nonetheless, travel she did, trying to fill up the emptiness in her life with new sights and new people. Her brother Arthur noted that "she would try anything, particularly if she had never attempted it before." And at a time when her life lacked purpose she did indeed seem willing to try anything, once even going up in a monoplane, against the advice of one of her many friends in the British military service, and declaring the experience "wonderful."

She continued her travels, going again to Egypt, where she had received a royal welcome from Coast Guard officers a few years before, and then on to India, where she was equally well received. She had always been attracted to men in uniform, and at least three old friends from the military proposed to her over the next few years. She refused all three offers of marriage and continued her aimless wandering. She paused in her travels long enough to plan and carry out an elaborate celebration for her parents' fiftieth wedding anniversary on December 21, 1907, despite the pain she felt in knowing that this was also the anniversary of her marriage to Willy Low. She was perpetual motion—but she accomplished nothing, blowing here and there like a whirlwind that did no harm but no good either.

When settlement of Low's will assured her financial security, she wrote to her mother that "I am just an idle woman of the world, with no real work or duties. I would like to get away from the world somewhere and work at sculpturing—start to do some work in life." It was her first expression of interest in art since she designed and forged wrought-iron gates for the entrance of the home she and Willy had bought in England. In 1911 she went to Paris to study sculpture under a tutor who encouraged her efforts but gave her no false hopes as to her abilities. She spent eight hours a day at her work and wrote "I am now at the height of bliss." Though she knew she lacked the talent that would make her a famous artist, she felt her sculpture would give her life "more serious interest."

Her interest in sculpturing did help her find new meaning in life, but not as she had anticipated. Returning to England, she met General Sir Robert Baden-Powell at a party featuring many well-known British military men. She had not expected to like him, since she'd felt his reputation as a hero of the Boer War was a bit overblown, but she found herself delighted with his company. They talked of sculpturing and sketching as well as soldiering and ceremony. And he told her of his work with the Boy Scouts, explaining how his use of young native boys in the noncombatant tasks involved in defending their village during the Boer War had convinced him that boys responded well to training that could make their lives fuller and more useful.

Here was a man who awakened her old desire to live a more meaningful life. Because of this man, 40,000 British boys were wearing a uniform that stood for a better way of life. Because of his caring, "guttersnipes" of London, poor farm boys of the Scottish hills, and sons of British lords and ladies could wear a uniform that emphasized their brotherhood rather than their differences. Daisy Low was impressed. And so was Robert Baden-Powell. They began to see more of each other, and Daisy found herself dreaming new dreams. She confided to her diary that "a sort of intuition comes over me that he believes I might make more out of life, and that he has ideas which, if I follow them, will open a more useful sphere of work before me in the future."

Baden-Powell did have ideas that were to open a "useful sphere of work." He told her about the Girl Guides, a group he had started when girls had written to tell him of their interest in Scouting. There were now 6,000 Girl Guides, with his sister Agnes leading the organization. Agnes needed help. Might Daisy be interested? Within weeks Daisy had organized the only seven girls within walking distance of the house she was renting in Scotland into a Girl Guides group.

She taught them childcare and nursing techniques. She taught them the Guide Promise and Laws, the history of the British flag, knot-tying, knitting, cooking, personal hygiene, and even signaling. Because most farm girls went into the city to find work and few thrived there, she taught the girls of her district skills that would allow them to earn money while staying at home. At her home the Girl Guides learned to spin so that they could get better prices than raw wool would bring. And she taught them to expect love and respect at a Girl Guide meeting—love and respect and a delicious teatime that was every bit as important to Daisy as the teas she had once given for the Prince of Wales and his friends.

Settling again in London, she soon had two patrols going there, and when she needed to leave for Georgia, she turned one of them over to a woman who tried to protest but reported that Daisy literally turned her deaf ear and refused to take no for an answer. It was a ploy that would serve her well in the years ahead. As one Englishwoman noted, "If you pleaded, as nearly everyone did, that you could not take up Guiding, that you had neither the capacity nor the time, in short, that it was quite impossible, she simply did not hear you!"

Daisy hardly had time to hear negative answers, for she and Baden-Powell were busy with plans for taking the movement abroad. They were both going to America at the same time and on the same ship, and they spent hours on board planning how Daisy would introduce Guiding to American girls. Occasionally a young woman named Olave Soames joined them in their conversations, enjoying their enthusiasm for the new undertaking. When Daisy got off in Jamaica and transferred to a ship that would take her to Savannah, Olave Soames and Robert Baden-Powell continued their conversations and fell in love before their ship reached New York.

Daisy, oblivious to Sir Robert's romantic adventure, continued with her plans to bring Guiding to America. She had hardly set foot in Savannah before she was calling on a friend who was principal of a girls' school there, telling her, "I've got something for the girls of Savannah and all America and all the world and we're going to start it tonight." Within days she had organized the first patrol, and on March 12, 1912, she wrote the name of Daisy Gordon, her 12-year-old niece and namesake, at the top

of the patrol's roster, thereby making her the first Girl
Guide in America. The patrol met in the carriage house
behind Daisy Low's house, and the girls were given the
building for their very own. They were proud of their uniforms and excited over the crafts and skills they learned at
meetings and on camping trips.

All over Savannah the news of the patrol's activities
began to bring more and more girls into the movement.
Here was an opportunity for Southern belles to don
bloomers and play basketball, to wear uniforms, take
nature hikes, and learn about girls and boys from other
lands. Here was a new way of learning and a new way of
having fun. For Daisy Low kept reminding her newly appointed leaders that Guiding was playing and that the happiness of the girls should always come first.

By late summer of 1912, little more than 18 months after
her first meeting with Robert Baden-Powell, Daisy was
totally involved in her work with Girl Guides and happier
than she had ever been in her life. Then on September 11
her happiness was shattered by the death of her beloved
father. For a while her own grief was hidden by her need
to care for her mother, who was devastated by William
Gordon's death. But eventually Daisy herself broke, though
secretly, telling everyone her arthritis had caused her to
spend time in a health resort, when in reality emotional
collapse had sent her there. Her health was likely not improved by news of Sir Robert's marriage to his shipboard
sweetheart, for it is quite likely that Daisy loved the
dashing Chief Scout whose ideas had given purpose to her
life.

Whatever her disappointment, she sent a warm letter of congratulations to the newlyweds, then pulled herself out of mourning and went to work for Girl Guides. The woman who had once drifted from place to place with no real sense of purpose had become a woman driven from place to place by her need to spread the message Sir Robert had entrusted to her. In her years of playing the fine lady, she had built a strong network of influential friends, a network that stretched across the United States. Now she called upon those friends, always with the same message— here is something for the girls of America. And she carried that same message to social workers such as Jane Addams of Hull House (see Chapter 1), stressing the impact that Girl Guiding could have upon the lives of the poor.

She tried, and failed, to merge her Girl Guides with the Campfire Girl organization already established in the United States, then took for her own group the name that she had intended to share—Girl Scouts of America. A new organization was underway, but one that never forgot its sisterhood with the Girl Guides in other parts of the world. By 1915 the new group had its own constitution, its own guidebook, and its first president—Juliette Gordon Low. She had soon enlisted the help of such famous women as Mrs. Thomas Alva Edison, Mrs. Cyrus McCormick, Mrs. John D. Rockefeller, Mrs. Herbert Hoover, and Mrs. Woodrow Wilson. She chose as well ordinary women in small towns across America and convinced all those she chose that Scouting was the most important thing they could possibly do to make the world a better place.

In 1917 President Wilson's announcement that the

United States was joining the war that had been raging in Europe made that work all the more urgent. The Girl Scouts of America offered their full support to the war effort; the First Lady became honorary president of the organization, and Girl Scouts across the nation participated in Red Cross work, started victory gardens, sold Liberty Bonds, and worked as nurses during the nationwide flu epidemic of 1918.

All the while, "Miss Daisy," as she was now known to the more than 7,000 girls who had taken up Scouting, was working to build an even stronger organization. By 1917 she had written a totally new guidebook, overseen the development of the official magazine that was to become *The American Girl*, guided regional groups in the establishment of camps for girls and for the training of leaders, helped design an official uniform, and helped establish a national headquarters. For years she herself had paid all the expenses of running the organization, including the salaries of the national staff, but Scouting was at last beginning to pay for itself.

The woman who had once spent thousands on a Parisian gown in which to be presented to Queen Victoria now wore a uniform that featured a khaki skirt and jacket, white shirt, black four-in-hand tie, gold braid across one shoulder, and a belt that supported a Scout knife, whistle, and tin drinking cup not unlike the knife and cup her grandmother Juliette Kinzie had worn on her trip across the plains to Chicago in the 1830s. And she wore the uniform proudly, not because she had to but, as one Scout leader put it, because she loved wearing it.

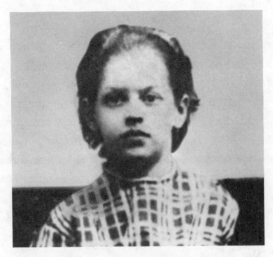

Juliette Gordon at 9

Juliette Gordon Low as president of the Girl Scouts of America

When she was first introduced to Sir Robert Baden-Powell she had thought of him as a man of war, but she had soon learned that he was a man dedicated to world peace. Though World War I temporarily shattered that dream, neither Sir Robert nor his friend Daisy were content to let it die. Olave Baden-Powell had become Chief Girl Guide of Britain, and in February of 1919 she and the Chief Girl Scout formed an international organization of Girl Scouts and Guides to foster the cause of world peace. By June of the following year the first International Conference was held in London, and in 1922 a World Camp was established.

By that time "Miss Daisy" had resigned as president of the Girl Scouts of America and had accepted the new title of "Founder." Her efforts were now directed toward bringing the World Camp to the United States in 1926. Others considered the task too monumental until Daisy confided to a few close friends that she would not be there to celebrate with them if they waited much longer. At that news, her followers set out to grant her wish, and in 1926 girls from around the world came to the United States for a ceremony of world peace. Sir Robert and Olave Baden-Powell joined Juliette Gordon Low in challenging the campers and their leaders to think of themselves as friends and neighbors, never again as enemies. It was the finest hour of Daisy Low's life.

That life was coming to a close. Though she had never admitted it to any but her closest colleagues and though her actions at the World Camp of 1926 never betrayed her pain, she had known for some time that she had cancer. On January 18, 1927, the founder of the Girl Scouts of

America died. She was buried in her full dress uniform, her tin cup and knife at her belt. In the pocket of her khaki jacket was a telegram from Girl Scout headquarters that she had received just before her death and had asked to have buried with her: "You are not only the first Girl Scout but the best Girl Scout of them all."

7

She Dared to Race Against Time

Margaret liked the feel of the room. It was small, but that made it just right for a ten-year-old. Already she was feeling comfortable and at home. She had a whole world all to herself up here on the third floor, tucked away in the attic of the large white farmhouse. She pressed her nose against the room's only window and studied the scene outside.

A branch from a giant elm reached out toward her, almost grazing the glass. Beyond the leaves she could see the greening field stretch into a patch of blueberry bushes that quickly gave way to tangled woods. They could find plenty to do out there, more than they'd found all winter in the house in Philadelphia. Before the day was over, she'd have to get Richard to go exploring with her.

Just now she wanted to unpack her books in whatever time she had left before her mother called her to help with Elizabeth and Priscilla or her grandmother called her to *lessons. Shoving the heaviest box across the hardwood floor and up to the bookcase, she sat cross-legged on the floor and tugged at the lid. Right on top were the notebooks she had been keeping on her two little sisters. No need to shelve the current one, for she was sure that Grandma's first assignment in this house would be to record their reactions to their new environment.*

She'd already done that once this year. She sighed as she put the first two volumes on the top shelf. Did anyone else move as often as they did? Not that she minded, for moving always meant new adventures. And she could feel at home almost any place, as long as she had her favorite things with her. But how did moving affect a three-year-old and an almost two-year-old? That was part of what Margaret was learning from the notebooks her grandmother had assigned her. Day after day she jotted down any significant behavior she observed in the two girls, and later she and her grandmother discussed her observations.

Now she'd see their reactions to life in the country. She flipped open the gray ledger book in her hand—it was nearly full. Like the other two volumes, it held her notes on how Elizabeth and Priscilla played and how they fought; on when they shared, what they shared, and with whom they shared; on each new word they learned and when and where they might have learned it. She flipped through her final Philadelphia entries: Cathedral. Marble. Statue. Elizabeth's vocabulary was full of city words. Here on the farm she and Priscilla would likely learn words for birds and trees and flowers.

"Margaret!"

It was time for lessons already. Margaret scrambled to

her feet and started into the hall, then dashed back into her
new room and scooped up the gray ledger book.

"I'm coming, Grandma," she called as she reached the
stairs. "And I've got the notebook."

"Good," called a voice from below. "Priscilla has found
an ants' nest."

An ants' nest. Margaret fairly flew down the last flight
of stairs. Through the parlor window she could see her
grandmother bending over Priscilla. The little girl was
pointing to something on the ground. As Margaret watched
the two of them, it was hard to tell which one was more
excited. She smiled. And this was the start of today's
schooling. Thank goodness for Grandma!

We can all be thankful for Margaret's grandmother. It
was largely through her influence that young Margaret
grew up to become the most famous note-taker of our
time and one of the most influential Americans of the
twentieth century. For Margaret Mead became an anthro-
pologist, one who studies the different ways people live.
She spent her life studying the cultures of South Sea
islanders, and through those studies she changed our way
of looking at the human race and showed us that the way
in which we behave is determined as much by the culture
in which we grow up as by any character traits we may
have inherited.

B orn in Philadelphia, Pennsylvania, on December 16,
1901, Margaret Mead was the eldest of five children,
one of whom died in infancy. Her father, Edward Sher-
wood Mead, was a professor of economics at the University

of Pennsylvania. Tall, strong, and stern, he left the super-
vision of Margaret and her sisters to their mother and
grandmother and concentrated his attention and ambitions
on his only son, Margaret's brother Richard. Though never
close to her father, Margaret was strongly influenced by
him and by his belief that "adding to the world's store of
knowledge is the most important thing anyone can do."

Small and gentle, but easily angered by injustice, Margaret's mother, Emily Fogg Mead, was a professional
woman who had been working on a doctoral degree when
Margaret was born and who continued her work throughout Margaret's infancy. Her field was sociology, or the
study of social relationships, and her special interest was
in the immigrant Italian families who lived in Hammonton,
New Jersey. Through all of Margaret's growing up years,
the Mead family spent spring and fall in Hammonton, so
her mother could be close to her work, and winters in
Philadelphia, so her father could be closer to the university.
By the time Margaret was ten, they had begun to spend
their summers at a farm in the Pennsylvania countryside,
and from that time onward, the family made at least four
moves a year.

Such a schedule might have posed schooling problems,
but the Meads handled that easily, if unconventionally.
Grandmother Mead, who had been both a schoolteacher
and a principal, lived with the family and devoted herself
to the education of her grandchildren. A small woman,
with dark, flashing eyes, strong opinions, and exciting
ideas, she was the single most dominant influence in Margaret's life. Convinced that learning was usually best accomplished on the go, she disapproved of any school that

kept children at their desks for long hours. She taught even the youngest children botany and biology by taking them into the field to study plants and animals, and she taught them the arts by taking them into the studios and craft shops of skilled painters and potters, woodworkers and weavers.

Some of young Margaret's most treasured hours were spent reading. But because both her parents thought too much reading was harmful to young eyes, she had to hide herself away to indulge her great love of books. She succeeded in this largely because no matter where the Meads moved, Margaret always claimed the most remote room in the house as her own. There she retreated in secrecy whenever she wanted quiet time with books. She wrote, too—vast quantities of poetry and stories and plays, which she then produced, directing her brother Richard and neighborhood children in roles written especially for them.

And then there were the notebooks, the records she kept under her grandmother's direction that charted the growth and development of her much younger sisters. In keeping those notebooks, she received the early training in listening, observing, recording, and analyzing that was to serve her so well when she began her work among the peoples on islands far removed from her girlhood homes.

During her teens, Margaret attended the local high school, though her grandmother continued to oversee her education, often criticizing and correcting the work of the classroom teachers. By this time Margaret was thinking seriously of what she would do with her life. At one time she considered being a nun, but her desire to have children, at least six of them, caused her to give up that idea in favor of becoming a minister's wife. Confident that she, like her mother and grandmother, could combine a family and a career, she cast about for a profession that interested her. Perhaps law, perhaps writing . . . but she was interested in her mother's work in sociology, too.

When her family could not afford to send her to Wellesley, her mother's college, she enrolled instead at DePauw University in Indiana, her father's alma mater, where she spent a disappointing freshman year. In September of 1920 she transferred to Barnard, the women's college of Columbia University in New York City, where she found an academic atmosphere that matched her earlier dreams. Being at Barnard also meant being closer to Luther Cressman, a tall, good-looking young ministerial student to whom she had been secretly engaged since her senior year in high school. During her last year at Barnard, still with no idea what her profession would be, she enrolled in a class taught by Franz Boas, the great anthropologist. That class gave her life exciting new direction.

In 1922 anthropology, the study of human cultures, was one of the youngest of the sciences. There were, in fact, not many anthropologists around. There were four graduate students studying under Boas at Columbia and only a handful studying at other universities in the United States. One of Boas's graduate assistants, a woman named Ruth Benedict, saw that young Margaret had the interests and the skills to make a fine anthropologist and urged her to turn to the new field. "Dr. Boas has nothing to offer but an opportunity to do work that matters," she told Mead one day, explaining that primitive cultures would soon give way to the modern civilization that was creeping into even the most remote areas of the world. There were no written records for many of those cultures. If they were not studied soon, the world would never have a record of their fascinating ways of life. It was a race against time. Mead was convinced. She shared her friend's sense of urgency.* "Anthropology has to be done now," Mead wrote. "Other things can wait."

In the spring of 1923 Margaret Mead got her degree from Barnard, began research for her master's degree in sociology —a study of the children of the very same Italian immigrant community her mother had studied years before— and married Luther Cressman. Her marriage was unorthodox from the beginning. To preserve her identity, Mead retained her own name rather than taking Luther's, an act so unusual for the time that it became a small item in many of the country's newspapers.

Even before her work for her master's degree was finished, Mead had decided to pursue a doctorate in anthropology. Professor Boas wanted her to study teenagers in the Indian tribes of the American southwest in order to discover whether or not the special problems of the adolescent years are unique to white American teenagers or are common in other cultures. Though fascinated by the idea of studying the adolescent, particularly the adolescent girl, Mead wanted to conduct the study among Polynesian peoples in the South Seas. Boas was aghast; Polynesia, he

---

* Ruth Benedict herself was to become a famous anthropologist, and she and Margaret Mead maintained a close friendship until Benedict's death in 1948.

said, was too remote, too isolated, definitely an unsafe area for a young woman to go to alone, as Margaret proposed to do. How could a woman not quite 5'3" tall and weighing less than 100 pounds have the stamina to endure the harsh life of the tropics? But what Margaret lacked in size, she made up for in determination. She was adamant; too many people were already studying the Indians. Too little work was being done in the Pacific where primitive cultures were quickly disappearing.

Mead and Boas came to a compromise. She would conduct her study among the Polynesian peoples of Samoa, an island group Boas considered relatively safe, since it was an American territory under the jurisdiction of the United States navy and therefore had some contact with the outside world. Other anthropologists remained skeptical. One of them, still unable to accept the work of women, told her she'd do better to stay home and have children herself, rather than go off to the South Seas to study them. Undaunted, Margaret began to prepare for her trip to Samoa. She planned to spend nine months in the field conducting her research. During that time her husband Luther would be studying in Europe. Boas secured a grant of $1,500 to support Mead's work in Samoa, and her father, proud of his daughter's ambition, promised to provide the money for her passage to Samoa, and, once her work was done, for a voyage around the far side of the world to meet Luther in Europe.

In the fall of 1925, having just received her Ph.D., Margaret set off for Samoa and Luther sailed for Europe. Traveling alone and living among Polynesian natives for nine months was indeed a daring undertaking for a 23-year-old woman. Her courage, she later said, came from "almost complete ignorance." She arrived in Pago Pago, the Samoan capital, alone and unmet. She had minimum baggage—a suitcase containing six cotton dresses, a pillow, six large notebooks, a Kodak camera, a flashlight, and a portable typewriter.

For six weeks she stayed in the naval hospital at Pago Pago absorbing what she could of the town and its people. She planned to become, as nearly as she could, a Samoan girl, "speaking their language, eating their food, sitting cross-legged on the pebbly floor," believing that "the only way in which I could be sure of knowing how a Samoan girl acted was to try to act that way myself." Learning to enjoy their foods—eel and rotten fish, green bananas, papaya, and taro—and to maintain herself for hours in a cross-legged position on an uncomfortable surface were difficult enough assignments. But learning the language— one of singsong syllables, completely unrelated to any Western language—was frustrating in the extreme. "I can't do it," she said to herself over and over. "I can't do it." Then suddenly one day she realized that she was saying "I can't do it" in Samoan. She knew she was ready.

With the advice of personnel at the hospital, she chose to do her study on Tau, one of the smallest of the Samoan Islands, working with the girls of three coastal villages. The villages were all within one-half mile of each other and had a total population of almost 1,000. They consisted of clusters of dwellings among groves of palm, breadfruit, and mango trees. The homes, each of which housed three or four families, were wall-less structures, set upon pillars of wood and topped with rounded thatched roofs of sugarcane. Mead herself lived with an American seaman, his wife, and their two children in the naval dispensary set up in one of the villages.

She began her work by mapping every house in the three villages and learning the number of girls in each house and how they were related to each other. In the end she focused her attention on 68 girls ranging in age from 9 to 20. Taking the name Makelita, she became, as she had planned, one of them. She dressed in their unisex *lavalava*, or sarong, walked barefoot with them, swam with them, and wove mats and baskets with them. Together she and the girls danced and chanted, worked in the sugarcane fields, and scoured the beaches for coral rubble. She listened to what each girl said about her life and her family, and all the while she filled her notebooks. Alert to every nuance of gesture and language, she applied all the methods she had learned in her grandmother's lessons. She observed, listened, recorded, analyzed. By adapting these methods, by choosing to study a culture through learning the language and living as a member of the community, she was setting the standards for the new science of anthropology.

In June of 1926 she left her Samoan friends on Tau and sailed to Europe to meet Luther. Together they returned to the United States. Back in New York, she went to work for the American Museum of Natural History. Her office was a tiny attic room with a view of the city below. Up there in the tower, two flights above the bustle of the museum, in a small domain that was to become her lifelong refuge, she turned her six fat notebooks into a book. *Coming of Age in Samoa* was a surprise best seller. Published in 1929 when Mead was 27 years old, the book immediately established her as a major figure in her field and instantly popularized the science of anthropology.

Through her careful research, Mead had discovered that the Samoan teenage girl was very different from her American counterpart. In the unhurried, relaxed existence of Tau, the adolescent years were the best years of a Samoan girl's life. She experienced no stress, no restlessness, no rebellion. The Samoan teenager suffered none of the tensions and unhappiness of the American, Mead said in *Coming of Age in Samoa*, because the Samoan girl had no sense of competition, did not form deep relationships with others her age, was free to move from family to family, and had no fears of adulthood, since she knew just what life would be when she grew up. Mead had found the answer to Boas's question. The turmoil of adolescence results not from our nature but from our culture.

Margaret Mead had shown that by studying another culture, we can learn much about our own. But there was more to do. Mead knew how quickly the cultures of the South Seas would disappear now that there was increasing contact with naval personnel and other visitors from the Western world. Already their languages, their music, their methods of hunting and fishing, and their arts and crafts were changing. There was not enough time, there were not enough workers in the field to give accounts of cultures before they vanished. In January 1929, even before *Coming of Age in Samoa* was published, Margaret Mead returned to the Pacific. This time she went to the Admiralty Islands north of New Guinea, and this time she did not plan to work alone. She joined forces with Reo Fortune, a psychologist whom she had met on the ship home from

Samoa and who, through her influence, had become increasingly interested in anthropology. Mead was by now divorced from Cressman. They had grown apart during their year's separation, and their future no longer held the promise it once had for Mead. Cressman had given up his ministry, and she had been told by a doctor that she could never have children. Divorce freed her to marry Fortune* and to begin their joint work with the Manus of the Admiralty Islands off New Guinea.

The Manus lived on the small island of the same name in houses built of sticks over the sea; their children learned to swim at the same time they learned to walk. It did not take Mead and Fortune long to discover that the Manus were very different from the carefree Samoans. The Manus were competitive, tense, and materialistic, and, not surprisingly, the Manu adolescent had much the same troubled passage to adulthood as did the American. The younger Manu children had almost no imaginative flair; the children could not draw, having no concept of color or pattern. In the six months Mead spent with them, she taught the children to express their thoughts in picture form, and she returned to the United States with over 35,000 pieces of children's art.

As it had been with the Samoans, Mead's relationship with the Manus was especially close. They called her "mother" and *pilapen*, or "female chief." As her canoe bore her away from their island toward the homebound

---

* Her second marriage proved hardly more durable than the first. Nor did her third. In reference to her three divorces, Mead said that her marriages never failed, they simply "got used up."

ship, the Manu men played the death roll on their drums. Back in her attic office at the museum in New York, Mead produced another book. In *Growing Up in New Guinea* she again used her findings to demonstrate that human behavior is more often the result of our culture than of our inborn nature.

Two years later, in 1931, Mead and Fortune returned to New Guinea, this time to study ways in which culture dictates the behavior of males and females. They intended to observe three tribes. By chance they chose three that, though living within 100 miles of each other, had vastly different cultures. The first tribe, the mountain Arapesh, were a peaceful, gentle people who responded readily to the needs of others. In this culture, both parents nurtured their children, and there was little difference in the behavior expected of men and of women. The second tribe, the Mundugumor, were headhunters. An aggressive people who abandoned unwanted infants, both the men and the women of the Mundugumor culture exhibited what modern culture labels "macho" behavior. The third tribe, the Tchambuli (known today as the Chambri), lived in a culture that reversed the traditional and stereotypical sex roles of the American society. Here the women earned the money, fished, gardened, and traded, while the men adorned themselves, gossiped, and were moody.

Returning to the United States early in 1934, Mead wrote *Sex and Temperament in Three Primitive Societies.* Her findings showed that the differences between what Americans considered appropriate male and female behavior were due not to human nature but to cultural conditioning. The way children were reared, the way certain kinds of behavior were rewarded or punished, the way heroes and villains were portrayed—those elements, and not innate characteristics, influenced the development of a child's temperament and personality. Furthermore, the way in which a society was organized determined the roles males and females were expected to play and therefore what talents and temperaments would be developed in children of the respective sexes.

In 1935, Mead was 33 years old. She was a world-famous scientist. With three major works published, she had already completed a lifetime's work. But she was far from satisfied. Reo Fortune chafed at her success. Their marriage did not survive their return from New Guinea. She divorced him shortly thereafter, planning to return to Bali, close by New Guinea, this time to work with Gregory Bateson, an English anthropologist she and Fortune had met on their last trip out. In 1936 she joined Bateson in Singapore, married him there, and began a two-year project in Bali, a beautiful island that was "sheer heaven for the anthropologist," according to Mead. It was home to one million people, all of whom spoke the same language. The villages were compact and located close together, and the culture was full of expressive ritual, with color, music, dance, and drama.

But there was a cloud on the horizon. By the late thirties, the world was moving toward war again, and Mead was well aware that a war would have great impact on primitive cultures in the Pacific. The race against time was on in earnest.

At this crucial moment, Mead herself briefly withdrew from that race. For when she came home from Bali, she was pregnant. She had had a lifetime interest in children, but doctors had said she would never have a child of her own, and she had resigned herself to that. Now she was ecstatic. She took a brief leave from the museum, and Mary Catherine Bateson was born late in 1939. She became one of the most studied children in history. From the beginning, Mead took notes and photographs of every one of her baby's actions—when she nursed, when she slept, when she cried, when she smiled, when she walked, when she spoke.

Gregory Bateson had to return to England at the outbreak of the European war in 1939, and Margaret Mead and Catherine shared a household with close friends so she could continue to travel and still leave the baby without worry. By 1941 the world was embroiled in the war that Mead marked as the pivotal point of our civilization. With the arrival of the atomic bomb, she said, humanity began a new age. "We are creating a new civilization," she wrote, one in which people throughout the globe experience events almost simultaneously. It was the very possibility of global destruction that fostered her theory of "the global village."

That theory was confirmed when, in 1953, 25 years after her first visit to the Manus, she returned to the Admiralty Islands, anxious to discover how time, World War II, and extensive contact with the West had affected the Manus. She could not have imagined the cultural change that awaited her. The Manus had advanced 5,000 years, leaping from the stone age to the atomic age, in a span of 25 years. The children of the Manus now lived in the same world as the children of the United States, bound by a technology that offered common foods, music, and clothing. When Mead had lived on Manus in 1928, the principal currency

Margaret Mead at 4

Margaret Mead at about 70

had been shells and dogs' teeth; now it was the Australian dollar. Diseases once treated by witchcraft were now treated by modern medical techniques. Physical labor and primitive science had given way to giant machines and complex technology.

Margaret Mead began to write of the new responsibilities placed on all peoples by such radical change. All nations of the planet were now affected by the dangers of stockpiling nuclear weapons and of polluting the earth, water, and air. All nations had to consider ways of shaping this newly emerging global civilization for the better. Mead did her part in this endeavor, serving on many national and international committees that spoke to such major issues as world nutrition, urban renewal, family planning, the rights of women and of minorities, mental health, and child care and education. She became a popular lecturer for both scientific and lay audiences.

"I enjoy everything I do," she had once said. And she did a lot. Even in advancing age, her energy never flagged. She gave sometimes as many as 100 lectures a year, and she wrote monthly columns for magazines, giving her advice and opinions on the myriad issues that attracted her interest.

She loved people and was an open, accessible celebrity. A stocky woman with a melodious voice and a grandmotherly appearance, she usually dressed very plainly. Rimless glasses framed her crisp blue eyes, and she always walked with the aid of her "thumbstick," a large forked stick she had picked up when she had broken her ankle during her first trip to New Guinea. She later rebroke that same ankle, and the walking stick became as much a necessity as an adornment.

In 1977 the American Museum of Natural History honored her by observing her seventy-fifth birthday with a week-long festival. She was still fully active; in fact, she told reporters she was "in the middle of several different things." But not much time was left to the energetic lady. Later that year cancer was discovered, and on November 16, 1978, Margaret Mead died.

She had lived, she once said, "neck-deep in the past," but the truth was that Margaret Mead brought her knowledge of the past to bear on modern questions, teaching us to see the connection between all peoples in all places at all times, reminding us that we are all one people, living in one world, a global village whose future depends upon the attitudes and actions of its inhabitants. And in so doing, the woman whom *Time* magazine once called "Mother to the World" has shown us the path to survival and made us acutely aware of modern society's own race against time.

8

She Dared to Insist
on Equality

"*Elizabeth Cady, you've had an hour to finish this stitch-ing! What have you been doing?*"

Twelve-year-old Elizabeth knew it was hopeless to try to hide the book she'd been reading. There it was on her lap in plain view, while discarded on the table beside her lay the tea towel her mother had set out as the day's exercise in embroidery. Slowly Elizabeth closed The Tales of King Arthur *and looked up at her mother. "I just wanted to finish this chapter. I was going to practice my stitches later this afternoon."*

"I did not say you could do stitchery at your leisure, Elizabeth. I said it was to be done now, this very hour. This is outright disobedience. Go immediately to your father's office and tell him what you've done."

Deliberately Elizabeth rose from the stiff-backed chair and crossed the room. A few steps down the hall brought her to the door that opened between the house and her

*father's law office. She knocked lightly, hoping she could
plead her case well enough to make her father see that it
was better to disobey by doing something worthwhile
than to obey, if that meant doing something senseless.*

*At her father's hurried "Yes?" she entered the room.
She was obviously interrupting him, for across the desk
from him, her back to Elizabeth, sat a woman dressed in
widow's black.*

"Yes, Elizabeth, is it important?"

"Not really, it can wait."

*"Well, perhaps it should. I'm busy right now. Mrs.
Campbell," he said to the woman who had turned to
Elizabeth as she entered the room, "I think you know my
daughter."*

*"Oh, yes," said the woman, wiping away her tears and
managing a weak smile, "Elizabeth has been out to my place
with her mother to pick up the eggs and such."*

*"Yes, I have," said Elizabeth with a quick, slight curtsy.
At her father's nod, she retreated to a footstool in the
corner of the book-lined office where she'd spent countless
hours before awaiting her father's attention.*

*Undistracted, he turned his gaze back to his client. "I
wish I could do more for you, Mrs. Campbell, but the law
clearly states that the farm was Mr. Campbell's to do with
as he pleased."*

*"But that's my place, Judge Cady. Mr. Campbell bought
it with my money. He can't just leave it to anyone he
wants."*

*"I'm afraid he can, Mrs. Campbell. It's his property
before the law to do with as he wants. And he gave it to*

his son. We can't contest that. I just wish there were more I could do."

"What will I do? Where will I go?"

The sturdy farm woman was now near collapse. Elizabeth, from her retreat in the corner, remembered the woman's sunny face as she had handed up the eggs and fresh produce to her mother on the buggy. She wanted to rush over and hug her, to share in some way in this injustice, but instead she sat without moving while her father accompanied Mrs. Campbell to the door, assuring her that he would talk to Mr. Campbell's son about making some arrangements for her future.

By the time he'd escorted Mrs. Campbell to her cart and returned to his desk, he'd forgotten that he still had Elizabeth to deal with. Elizabeth weighed her position for only a moment. She could sit quietly in the corner and avoid bringing trouble down upon herself. But to do that would be to ignore the injustice that had just been revealed.

"Father, if that's Mrs. Campbell's farm, then why won't you do anything?"

Startled, then angered, her father rose. *"It's the law, Elizabeth, plain and simple. Married women cannot hold property. That is not her farm. It was her husband's, and now it's his son's. But that's not your concern—nor is it mine. My concern is your behavior. What have you done now?"*

"Nothing, father," Elizabeth answered. How could she talk to him of embroidery, preoccupied as she was with the injustice she had just witnessed?

And Elizabeth Cady Stanton was to remain preoccupied with injustice for the rest of her life. It was she who, in the *middle of the nineteenth century, gathered together the forces that were to become the movement that sought equal rights for women.*

Elizabeth Cady, the fourth of six children, was born on November 12, 1815, in Johnstown, New York, a small town near Albany. Her father, Daniel Cady, was an able lawyer, a New York state legislator, and a justice of the state supreme court. Her mother, Margaret Livingston Cady, was from a well-known and well-thought-of family in the area, and she was determined to raise her children in the strict discipline of the day. Her one son was given all the benefits of a good education, and her daughters all the benefits of good domestic training. But Elizabeth, a carefree, fun-loving child, had little interest in the domestic arts and was keenly aware of the difference in her parents' expectations of their son and of their daughters. Those expectations ended with the sudden death of Eleazer at age 22. When Elizabeth, then 11 years old, attempted to comfort her father, she was dashed by his response: "Oh, my daughter, I wish you were a boy."

From that day, Elizabeth set out to prove to him that a daughter was as good as a son. It seemed to her that in order to do so, she had only to become "learned and courageous." To be learned, she took up Greek; to be courageous she turned to horseback riding. But excelling in both was not enough. Judge Cady's response when she brought home a first prize in Greek in competition with the boys at Johnstown Academy was an echo of his earlier words: "Ah, you should have been a boy."

Elizabeth herself might occasionally have held that opinion, for she spent much of her growing-up time in her father's office and overheard many unsettling conversations like the one between her father and Mrs. Campbell. Such conversations provided constant reminders of the unjust position the law assigned to women. When a woman married, her husband gained title to any property she owned and any wages she earned. To him fell guardianship of their children. But if the law was unjust toward women, social customs were even harsher. Thought to be physically and intellectually incapable of higher education, women were not allowed access to colleges. Nor were they allowed to enter the professions and trades. Domestic labor, work in textile mills, and teaching were by and large the only jobs open to them. For hours at a time, Elizabeth Cady argued the law and the custom with her father and with the students who read law under him.

Since no American colleges were open to women when Elizabeth finished Johnstown Academy in 1830, she entered Troy Female Seminary, reputed to be one of the country's leading girls' schools. Two years later, having completed her work at the school, she was at loose ends. There was little for an educated woman to do in 1832 but marry or teach, and she was not yet willing to do either. Over the next eight years she read law with her father and became a student of legal and constitutional history, but she knew that as a woman she could never practice law.

Through visits in the home of a cousin who was active in the Underground Railroad, she became interested in the abolitionist, or anti-slavery, movement. It was there that she met Henry Stanton, a man ten years her senior and an active abolitionist. Attracted to the man and to his cause, she married him in 1840. In that wedding ceremony, the bride vowed only to "love and honor" her husband, omitting the promise "to obey." Nor did she ever sign her name as Mrs. Henry B. Stanton, which would have been the custom of the day. Convinced that no woman should lose her own identity in marriage, she was always to be Elizabeth Cady Stanton.

On their honeymoon the Stantons sailed for England and the World's Anti-Slavery Convention in London. There Elizabeth Cady Stanton met Lucretia Mott, a well-known leader of the abolitionist movement in America and an official delegate to the convention. The two women spent much time together, particularly after delegate Mott was denied her seat in the convention because she was a woman. Sitting on park benches in London the women talked of the slavery that oppressed women as well as black people and made plans to hold a meeting publicizing the unequal social and legal status of women when they returned to America.

But upon her return home, life drew Elizabeth Cady Stanton in a different direction. After two years in Johnstown, where Henry studied law under Judge Cady and where their first son was born, the Stantons moved to Boston in 1843. There Elizabeth became happily involved in running her household and tending three active little boys. For despite having begrudged the childhood hours given to learning the domestic arts, she enjoyed housekeeping. She enjoyed mothering, too, though she made no secret of the fact that she was not raising her children according to the accepted practices of the day. At a time when infants were tightly swaddled in clothes and blankets to restrict their movement and guard their energy for growth, Mrs. Stanton left her babies free to flail their arms and legs at will, proclaiming that in free activity they grew, and grew strong. Remembering the rigid discipline of her own childhood, she was determined to persuade, not force, her children to do the right thing.

But housework and mothering were not her only activities. In Boston, surrounded by friends of like interests and by opportunities to see and do all manner of things, she visited museums, went to lectures and concerts, and felt fulfilled. That sense of contentment ended in 1847 when Henry Stanton moved the family to Seneca Falls, a small town not far from Elizabeth's childhood home. Without the diversions of Boston, the responsibilities of housekeeping and mothering that had once seemed enjoyable became drudgery without relief. Her husband, now involved in politics, was free to come and go at will, while she was confined to a house and to a family's schedule. Isolated and oppressed, she herself turned to politics, at least to the degree she could while staying close to home. Using her father's and her husband's influence, she wrote letters to state legislators in Albany, urging them to pass the Married Woman's Property Act, which would give married women such as Mrs. Campbell the right to own property. When that act became law in early 1848, she felt it to be a personal triumph.

Then, in the summer of 1848, eight years after their meeting in London, Elizabeth Cady Stanton heard that Lucretia Mott was coming to Seneca Falls to visit her sister. The women met again, and Stanton poured out all her dissatisfactions with her role as housewife and mother, noting that there was injustice enough to turn any woman's thoughts "from stockings and puddings." Lucretia Mott was sympathetic to all she heard, the long-ago scheme to have a meeting to discuss women's grievances was revived, and plans for a "Woman's Rights Convention" were soon underway. A notice was published in the Seneca Falls paper, and Elizabeth Cady Stanton began to draw up a body of resolutions to present to the conference. She called her paper a Declaration of Sentiments, and she patterned it after the Declaration of Independence.

"We hold these truths to be self-evident," she wrote, "that all men and women are created equal." Like the national declaration of 72 years before, her statement listed 18 points, grievances that she'd first become aware of years before while listening to her father counsel his clients and that had become even more bothersome as she grew older and felt the injustice in her own life. Her resolution called for giving women the right to own property, the right to their earnings and to the guardianship of their children, the right to equal pay for equal work, the right to higher education, the right to enter the trades and professions that had never been open to them, and the right to bring suit and to appear as witness in a court of law.

These and related resolutions were all very familiar to anyone who had ever considered reform, but one of Elizabeth Cady Stanton's resolutions had never been publicly voiced before. It was shocking to everyone to whom she showed it, even to Lucretia Mott, and particularly to her father and her husband. The Declaration of Sentiments called for the right for women to vote! Though for Stanton that right was never more than one of a long list of reforms that women must achieve for full equality, suffrage was to be the rallying cry for women's rights for the next 72 years, until the Nineteenth Amendment gave women the vote in 1920.

Lucretia Mott and Elizabeth Cady Stanton hardly knew what turnout to expect for their "convention," and they were astounded when on July 19, 1848, 300 people, men and women, gathered at the little Wesleyan Chapel in Seneca Falls. There had been workers for women's rights before 1848, but they were scattered and isolated. At Seneca Falls those workers found their leader—Elizabeth Cady Stanton—and their program—the Declaration of Sentiments. A movement had been launched. From that small, crowded chapel on a warm July day, the feminist movement would inch its way across the country and across the next century and a half to bring equal rights to women.

The Seneca Falls Convention, her first exposure to public life, was a triumph for Stanton, but she suffered for her success. Her father dissociated himself from her stance and briefly disinherited her. The public heard the Declaration of Sentiments ridiculed in newspapers and from pulpits. But Stanton had seen that others shared her outrage at injustice, and she busied herself now in doing what she could to bring about change. She was a woman of almost boundless energy, and that energy, plus her infectious need to right wrongs, attracted people to her. Her home in Seneca Falls became an open house, a meeting ground for all who would join in her crusade to win women's rights.

Through letters, petitions, and articles, she made known

her views. Women were not only equal to men in physical and mental abilities, they were actually superior; only the traditional suppression of the female had caused any measurable differences. If boys and girls were treated the same way, if their education and their exercises were identical, if they were given similar training and wore similar clothes, then physically and mentally they would develop equally. When the abilities of women were fully developed, their equality could no longer be denied.

But while she had infinite confidence in the natural capabilities of women, Elizabeth Cady Stanton couldn't close her eyes to the obvious fact that the majority seemed to wear their chains with pleasure. She held that no improvement was possible until women had more respect for themselves, realized their unequal status before the law and by custom, and worked to correct the obvious injustices. Not until women had entry to all trades and professions, not until they could support themselves, afford their own housing, and hold their own bank accounts, would they control their own lives.

As Elizabeth Cady Stanton saw it, the whole question of control of one's own life turned on the quality of a marriage, since a woman's marriage was so often the center of her life. She called for legal equality within marriage and social equality in family roles, yet she saw that under present conditions all too many marriages were, for wives, little more than a long, hard struggle to make the best of a bad bargain. For this reason, she proclaimed that, in the struggle for equal rights, laws providing for easy divorce were as necessary as laws granting women the right to vote.

In her own life, in her own home, Elizabeth Cady Stanton applied everything she proclaimed. Though she envied her husband the freedom and travel afforded by his law practice and political activities, and though she was often frustrated by her confinement to the house and to the children, she used his absence to consolidate her own position and to raise her five sons and two daughters in absolute equality. When the town of Seneca Falls provided an after-school sports program for boys, but not for girls, the barn behind the Stanton house was equipped as a gymnasium where the girls and their friends exercised and competed in the same fashion as did the boys.

Their activities in the gym were made easier because Cady Stanton believed in comfortable, practical clothing for women and girls. She became one of the earliest and staunchest advocates of "bloomers," an outfit named for Amelia Bloomer, a Seneca Falls friend and neighbor. Bloomers, a pair of pantaloons worn under a long tunic, allowed for ease in doing housework, in caring for children, and in walking unpaved streets—all in all, an outfit much to be preferred over long, heavy skirts, which could weigh as much as 12 pounds, and tight, restrictive stays at the waist and bustline.

After several years of public ridicule for her dress, however, Elizabeth Cady Stanton gave up her bloomers and returned to conventional garments. If her appearance in bloomers was so shocking and so upsetting to people that it detracted from her work to win women's rights, then far better to give up a comfortable style of dress and keep the public's attention on the issues at hand.

In the early days, Cady Stanton often felt as if she stood

alone in that attempt. There were those who offered what support they could, but most people, even women, were afraid of her ideas. She was lovable, she was stimulating, but she was far too radical. Then one day in 1851 Amelia Bloomer introduced her to Susan B. Anthony, a friend who was visiting Seneca Falls, a friend who was very interested in the temperance movement but who had not yet become involved in the movement for women's rights. It was a fateful meeting, bringing together the two women who would dominate the fight for sexual equality over the next half century.

No two women could have been so different in person and personality, yet so close in cause and in friendship. Elizabeth Cady Stanton was attractive, short and stout, motherly, and merry. Susan B. Anthony was at best plain, tall and gaunt, reserved, even grim. But together the two of them became as one force. "In thought and sympathy we are one, in the division of labor we exactly complement each other," Stanton said of their relationship. Anthony had a talent for organization and a love of research and fact finding. Stanton had a flair for leadership and a talent for inspiring others, both in speech and in writing.

But that flair, at least in the early days of their friendship, was limited by Stanton's commitment to home and to family. Anthony, a spinster, was rootless and free to travel. Periodically she moved in with the Stantons, sitting up late in the evening with her friend, planning the ways by which they could advance the cause. Each woman brought her different abilities to the task. Anthony put the facts before Stanton and Stanton fashioned them into stirring words. "Our speeches may be considered the united product of our two brains," Stanton said. "I forged the thunderbolts and she fired them."

It was not always Anthony who went off to give the speeches, however. At times she stayed behind and cared for the Stanton children while their mother spoke to legislative committees or women's clubs or anti-slavery conventions. "We made it a matter of conscience to accept every invitation to speak on every question in order to maintain woman's right to do so," Cady Stanton said.

In 1854 she was invited to speak before the New York state legislature, the first woman to address that group. She spoke persuasively for the rights of married women, for extending to them the right to their own wages and the right to the legal guardianship of their children. And she rejoiced for herself and for all other women of the state when, in 1860, those rights were finally granted them by law.

But in 1860 the United States was broken apart by the Civil War, and Elizabeth Cady Stanton, Susan B. Anthony, and other leaders in the crusade for women's rights gave up their campaign for the duration of the war in order to concentrate their efforts on the freeing of the slaves and the preservation of the Union. When Abraham Lincoln's Emancipation Proclamation granted freedom only to those slaves living in the Confederate states, Stanton and Anthony formed the Woman's National Loyal League to press for freedom for all blacks. Yet at the close of the Civil War, the two women vigorously opposed the passage of the Fourteenth and Fifteenth Amendments that would grant full citizenship to all black males. They felt clearly betrayed that black men were being given the vote and full equality when women of all races were still being denied those rights.

In 1869 Stanton and Anthony formed the National Woman's Suffrage Association, an organization into which they poured all their efforts to secure the vote for women. For the next 21 years, Stanton was to serve as the president of the association. Her family and home now demanded less of her attention, and partly to have a platform for her views and partly to provide for her children's college education, she went on the national lecture circuit, spending the decade of the seventies crossing the United States, speaking out for women's rights.

A persuasive orator, she became one of the most popular speakers on the circuit. A handsome, if portly, woman with rosy cheeks, twinkling blue eyes, and neatly curled white hair, she was always stylishly dressed in black. Her audiences took to her, applauding the woman even when they did not applaud her cause. Her openness, her warm and witty presence, and the fact that she was the mother of seven endeared her to audiences and perhaps in the end did more than her words to convince her hearers of woman's ability to take her place as a full member of society.

In 1887 Henry Stanton died, and Elizabeth Cady Stanton, now 72 years of age, began to curtail some of her activity. She spent more time now with her children, two of whom were living in Europe, and turned most of her energy to writing. Over the years of the eighties, she and Anthony had worked on the first three volumes of *The History of Woman's Suffrage*, a record of the earliest days of the struggle. But during that time the two friends had

Elizabeth Cady at 20

Elizabeth Cady Stanton at 60

begun to drift apart in their philosophy and their strategy. Stanton was always mindful of the injustices suffered by women in all spheres, not just the political one, and she sought reform in many areas—in woman's position in the home, in education, in religion, and in society in general. To Anthony it was a single-minded cause: women must have the right to vote.

The rift between the women was widened with the publication of *The Woman's Bible* in 1895. Long disillusioned by the role played by organized religion in suppressing the development of women, Cady Stanton wrote *The Woman's Bible* to explain the biblical passages that were used to limit women's status. The book was denounced, not only because Stanton spoke against widely held religious opinion, but also because a woman had dared to comment on the Bible at all. As bloomers had, long years before, shocked both supporters and opponents of the feminist movement, now so too did *The Woman's Bible*, and Susan B. Anthony quickly dissociated herself from it.

But not from its author. Cady Stanton had always been a radical among them, had always pushed the movement to the limits in its demands, and Anthony, more than any other feminist, never ceased to appreciate her friend's unequaled contribution to the cause. Late in 1895, on the occasion of Elizabeth Cady Stanton's eightieth birthday, Anthony organized a gala celebration, "a woman's festival" at the Metropolitan Opera House in New York City. She called it a Reunion of the Pioneers and Friends of Woman's Progress, but the evening, shared by 6,000 people, was clearly a testimony to one person. Elizabeth Cady Stanton

sat center stage while women who represented every possible line of women's work—medicine, the arts, education
—gave testimony to what Stanton had accomplished and to
the difference her work had made in their lives. By now a
woman of some 240 pounds, the guest of honor was unable
to stand for any length of time, and her remarks at the end
of the ceremony were brief and uncustomarily modest: "I
am well aware that these demonstrations are not so many
tributes to me as an individual as to the great idea I rep-
resent. . . ."

Stanton remained as active leader of the movement for
another seven years. At her death in 1902 at the age of
86, she was the Grand Old Woman of America, forgiven
for her radicalism, loved for herself and for what she had
done to change the national attitude toward woman's
ability and woman's equality. She had been a torchbearer,
a learned and courageous leader who had dared to question
and, for half a century, had prodded others into question-
ing, too.

And though it would be years after her death before
women had the right to vote and even more years before
they had access to all the nation's universities and to the
trades and professions and before they had equality in their
roles in marriage and the family, Elizabeth Cady Stanton
had brought many Americans to an awareness of a basic
injustice in their society and had set into motion the forces
that would eventually bring about the reforms she had
spent her life endorsing.

9

She Dared to Be an Athlete

"*Look, it's gettin' too dark. We can't see good. Besides, we'll get a lickin' for bein' so late.*"

"*One more inning, just one more. She's got her ups again, and we want to see if she can do it one more time.*"

"*Bet she can't. She's just lucky. Besides, anybody could do it.*"

"*Well, if anybody could do it, how come you ain't done it?*"

"*Maybe I just don't need to go around showin' off like that.*"

"*Showin' off? Why, she can't hardly help bein' so good. She ain't showin' off. She's just bein' herself.*"

"*Yeah, well I don't even like her playin' with us. Girls ought to be doin' girl things.*"

"*Yeah, well you tell her that. Anyhow, quit wastin' our time. Come on, one more inning!*"

One half of the ragged group of ballplayers moved onto the crudely carved diamond on the vacant lot on Doucette

133

Avenue and took up their positions. The others flopped to the ground off the first-base line and watched as one of their number picked up the bat that lay across the plate and mindlessly took a practice swing.

There was little to set apart the slat-thin figure at bat from the boys she played with. At age 12, there was no difference between her form and that of her playmates. But there was one notable difference—the girl seemed a bit too good for the competition she found on the sand-lots in Beaumont, Texas. And she seemed to have a need to prove that. She pounded the bat against the bare spot at her feet and looked to the boy who stood in the pitcher's well-worn groove. Her own teammates were now abuzz with the excitement. This batter had already blasted four home runs. No one else in their memory had ever even approached such greatness.

"Come on, Mildred. This is it."

"It's gettin' too dark. You won't get another try."

"Come on, you're good enough. Come on, show 'em!"

How good was she? What more could she show them? They watched in awe as she unleashed her bat at the first pitched ball and propelled it in a graceful arc across the lot and onto the roof of the streetcar barn that loomed at the edge of their ballfield.

"Babe, man, she's Babe Ruth! There's no one else can do that. Hey, Babe, think you can make the big leagues?"

"Yeah, I prob'ly can, at least I'm sure gonna try," Babe Didrikson shot back at she loped triumphantly down the first-base line.

She never did, though. As an athlete, as a woman athlete, Babe Didrikson Zaharias was just too far ahead of her time to have played professional baseball. But because of her natural ability, her determination, and her courage, she did make many other breakthroughs for women in sports.

Today when girls play Little League ball and women drive in the Indianapolis 500, it's hard to believe that at one time being a girl meant that you had little chance to participate in athletics. But when Babe Didrikson was growing up, many people even believed that it was unhealthy for girls to develop athletic skills. Fortunately, Babe was happily unaware of what she should or shouldn't do and thoroughly enjoyed doing what she could. She worked out on the backyard gym set her father had rigged for his children out of a broomstick and his wife's discarded flatirons. She raced her sister Lillie down the block, hurdling the hedges that divided every yard from its neighbor, while Lillie ran the flat course of the sidewalk. Though she was two years younger than Lillie, Babe always won those matches. She was physically gifted and she was fiercely competitive, traits that weren't admired in girl children.

Born in Port Arthur, a small Texas town, on June 16, 1911, Mildred Didriksen was the sixth of seven children of Ole and Hannah Didriksen, both Norwegian immigrants.* As a girl in Norway, her mother had been an accomplished skater and skier. Her father, a ship's carpenter, had settled his family in Texas several years before Mildred's birth.

---

* As an adult, Babe changed the spelling of her last name because she thought Didrikson was closer to the Norwegian form.

When Mildred was just four years old, a violent hurricane destroyed the Didriksen home in Port Arthur, and the family moved to nearby Beaumont. There in the South End of that raw Texas town, the young Didriksens grew up in an environment that was to have a profound effect on Mildred's attitudes and abilities. The South End was a tough neighborhood where youngsters learned to compete early. To survive, to succeed, one learned to be aggressive, to be competitive, and Mildred Didriksen learned well.

The family was poor, but so was everyone else they knew, and young Mildred never thought of herself as "deprived." Her beloved Mama and Poppa provided for all her needs, and she earned extra spending money with part-time jobs such as mowing lawns and sewing gunny sacks for a penny a sack. Though never an apt student, she stood out in every sport she turned to. As a second grader she became the marbles champion of Magnolia Elementary School, besting a sixth grade boy in the final round. Never content to compete against girls, who seemed to her to care little about proving themselves, she played with the boys. And it was the boys who were sufficiently awed by her home run production in sandlot games to give her the nickname of all America's idol—Babe Ruth. She took it for her own, and from that day was known only as Babe.

Wiry, thin and achieving her full height of 5'6" only in her mid-teens, Babe had astonishing strength for her size. Beatrice Lytle, her high school gym teacher, recalled years later how "her muscles flowed when she walked. She had a neuromuscular coordination that is very, very rare." And Babe practiced. She devoted herself almost single-mindedly to improving her skill in whatever sport held her interest at the moment, and she excelled in every sport she ever tried. She batted over .400 in the Beaumont city softball league, could punt a football 75 yards, had a 170 bowling average, won tennis tournaments and diving championships, and swam short-distance events in times close to world records. She even gave billiards exhibitions.

But throughout her high school years her greatest interest was basketball. Though small, she was quick and cocky, and news of her exploits reached Colonel Melvin J. McCombs, a retired army officer who was director of the women's athletics program at Employers Casualty Company, an insurance firm in Dallas. At that time there were no university or professional sports programs for women in America, and older girls played for "industrial" teams. Dozens of such teams existed in the United States in the thirties, most of them sponsored by oil and insurance companies who benefited from the publicity generated by the games.

Colonel McCombs went to Beaumont to scout the 18-year-old sensation, overcame her parents' objections, and convinced Babe to go to work for Employers Casualty. In February 1930, in the middle of her senior year in high school, Babe Didrikson left Beaumont for Dallas, where for $75 a month she became an 86-word-a-minute typist for Employers Casualty and a high-scoring player for the company's Golden Cyclones. That very year she carried the team to the finals of the women's national tournament, and the next year she led them to the national championship. Often scoring 30 or more points a game in an era when 20 points was a respectable team score, Babe Didrikson was an All-American in 1930, 1931, and 1932.

The three years in Dallas were vitally important in Babe's development as an athlete. Under the guidance of Colonel McCombs she trained with the proper equipment and under professional coaching. Noting Babe's restlessness at the end of each basketball season, McCombs decided she needed an off-season outlet for her talent and energy and took her to a track meet in the spring of 1931. She was hooked. She had followed with interest the 1928 Olympics in Amsterdam, the first to include women's track and field events, and she knew that the 1932 Olympics would be held in Los Angeles. She saw her chance, and she began training in earnest.

In July of 1932 the national Amateur Athletics Union meet held in Evanston, Illinois, served not only to decide the national championships but also to qualify American athletes for the Los Angeles Games. The team that the Golden Cyclones sent to the meet in Evanston consisted of one person—Babe Didrikson. Pitted against the country's best female athletes in eight events, Babe raced through her events in a span of three hours in what one reporter called "the most amazing series of performances ever accomplished by any individual, male or female, in track and field history." Babe came in first in six of the eight events—in the hurdles, the javelin, the high jump, the baseball throw, the shot put, and the long jump—and she set world records in the first four. Fourth in the discus, she failed to place only in the 100-yard dash. The amazing one-woman team earned 30 points, defeating the second-place team, which had 22 members competing, by an eight-point margin.

Though Babe's performance at Evanston qualified her

to compete in all five Olympic track and field events open to women, the rules of the time limited her participation to three Olympic events, and she chose to enter the hurdles, the javelin, and the high jump. In early August of 1932, wearing America's colors at the Tenth Olympiad in Los Angeles, Babe Didrikson won two gold medals—running the 80-meter hurdles in 11.7 seconds and tossing the javelin 143′ 4″, 11 feet farther than any woman had ever tossed it before. Though her 5′ 5¼″ leap in the high jump tied her with the winner, she had to settle for a silver medal in that event. Her "diving" technique, the western roll that later became standard form, was ruled illegal by the Olympic judges, who rather than disqualifying her simply placed her second.

Grantland Rice, one of the country's most respected sportswriters, summed up the totality of Babe's Olympic accomplishments. "She is an incredible human being. She is beyond all belief until you see her perform. Then you finally understand that you are looking at the most flawless section of muscle harmony, of complete mental and physical coordination the world of sport has ever known. There is only one Babe Didrikson, and there has never been another in her class—even close to her class."*

Babe returned to Dallas to a hero's welcome on August 11, 1932. The mail plane that brought her circled low over the city while whistles and sirens sounded in the streets below. A crowd of 10,000 people greeted her at Love Field. Tanned and slender, she stepped off the plane, carry-

---

* At the Olympics a reporter had asked Babe, "Is there anything at all you haven't played?" Her reply: "Yes, dolls."

ing three javelins. A band struck up "Hail to the Chief."
At 21 years of age, Babe held five national or world records
and was America's new sports idol.*

But the fame died quickly. America, in the middle of a
depression, did not dwell long on Olympic heroes. Babe
was disillusioned; she craved attention. In the next few
years she permitted herself to be exploited in publicity
stunts. She had always been full of foolishness and pranks;
now she gave way to outright braggadocio. At one time she
seriously considered an offer to sprint against a race horse;
another time she challenged Babe Ruth to a sparring match
in New York. She did a vaudeville act at the Palace Hotel
in Chicago, playing the harmonica, a talent she had developed as a girl in Beaumont, while running on a tread-
mill on stage. She organized the Babe Didrikson All-Stars,
a basketball team made up of both men and women that
played throughout the Midwest. She joined the House of
David baseball team, a colorful group of bearded men who
toured America each summer. During spring training in
1934, she even pitched and played third base for several
major league baseball teams—the St. Louis Cardinals, the
Philadelphia Athletics, and the Cleveland Indians. She drew
crowds, but she also drew derision. People did not know
what to think of a woman who so excelled in what had
traditionally been a man's world. They ridiculed her for
her competitiveness, her aggressiveness, her excellence.
They called her a "muscle moll," a freak. She was, in fact,

---

* Babe's records: 11.7 seconds in the 80-meter hurdles, 143′4″ in the
javelin, 5′5¼″ in the high jump (co-holder), 18′8½″ in the broad
jump, and 272′2″ in the baseball throw.

a loving, generous, and gentle young woman, full of fun and energy. She was "toughened," she said, as all girls in sports must be, but she was not "tough."

She was an ambitious, accomplished young athlete who seemed to have lost her way. And then she rediscovered golf. It was a sport she had played occasionally at home in Beaumont, but one she had once described as "silly." While in Los Angeles for the Olympics, she had played a round of golf with Grantland Rice and a group of other sportswriters, but the game had not seemed sufficiently challenging. Then in 1934 she saw an exhibition match played by Bobby Jones, the world-famous golfer. She was impressed—impressed enough to take her life's savings of $1,800 and travel with both her parents to Los Angeles to pursue golfing in earnest. There she was given free lessons by Stanley Kertes, one of the sport's most talented teachers.

Having depleted her savings, but having learned the game's basic techniques from one of the best, Babe returned to Dallas shortly thereafter and took up her old job with Employers Casualty. Colonel McCombs arranged for her membership in the Dallas Country Club, and there she began a vigorous practice schedule, spending hours on the driving range and putting greens, binding her blistered palms against the bleeding. "Practice and concentration—and more practice and concentration—there are no short cuts," she said.

In 1934, the very year she took up the sport, she entered her first golf tournament, scoring a 77 in the first round. Texas newspapers headlined her performance: "Babe Didrikson is still America's wonder girl athlete." At 23, the

Babe Didrikson at about 10

Babe Didrikson Zaharias in her early 30s

Babe was back, and commanding a brand new sport. The next year she entered the Texas women's state championship. She won it, of course.

In 1938, while playing in the Los Angeles Open, usually a male-only tournament, but one for which she qualified, she met George Zaharias, a nationally known professional wrestler. Babe was captivated. So was George. They were married that same year. George became Babe's manager and promoter, and Babe Didrikson Zaharias went on to dominate women's golf for the next 20 years.

But she did more than dominate the sport; she changed it. She brought power and excitement to the game, driving the ball 300 yards off the tee and breaking 70, an amazing feat at that time. And through it all she entertained the galleries with quips and tricks. In 1946 she won the British Women's Amateur championship, becoming the first American to do so. The tournament was held in Edinburgh, Scotland, and the Scots were charmed with the new champion. Babe donned a tartan and danced a fling for the galleries. One of the thousands who had followed her around the course told her, "Ah, lass, we won't be forgettin' you for a while."

In 1948 she became one of the founding members of the Ladies Professional Golf Association (LPGA), a group dedicated to the promotion of women's golf. The sport was sorely in need of promotion, since there were only two professional tournaments a year open to women at that time. It was largely due to Babe's talent and personality that the LPGA was able to succeed in its efforts. Her flair and color drew the galleries, and her power astonished them.

In all, Babe Didrikson won some 84 golf tournaments. She won 14 of them in a row, quite a feat, considering the fact that two consecutive wins on the professional tour today constitute a "streak." By 1953, she had won every major golf title available to her, including three national titles and four world championships. She was named Associated Press's Woman Athlete of the Year six times in all and in 1950 was acclaimed their Woman Athlete of the Half Century. She had finally gained the nation's affection as well as its attention, and her fabled career had changed America's attitude toward women in sports.

In 1953 that career was threatened when doctors discovered that she had cancer and performed radical surgery. Undaunted, Babe came back 15 months later to win her third U.S. Women's Open title by 12 strokes, a record margin. She went on to win four more golf tournaments in 1954, but by the next spring the malignancy had recurred. Babe's endurance and fine physical condition combined to cause a long, slow death. She had finally met an opponent she could not defeat.

On September 27, 1956, at age 45, Babe Didrikson Zaharias died. President Dwight D. Eisenhower opened his press conference that morning with a tribute to his friend: "She was a woman who in her athletic career certainly won the admiration of every person in the United States, [and] all sports people over the world." But Grantland Rice had probably already said it best: "The Babe . . . is without question, the athletic phenomenon of all time, man or woman."

INDEX